Initiation

NIK VALENTINE

Dreamspinner Press

Published by
Dreamspinner Press
5032 Capital Circle SW
Suite 2, PMB# 279
Tallahassee, FL 32305-7886
USA
http://www.dreamspinnerpress.com/

Initiation
© 2014 Nik Valentine.

Cover Art
© 2014 Christy Caughie.
Cover content is for illustrative purposes only and any person depicted on the cover is a model.

ISBN: 978-1-62798-355-6
Digital ISBN: 978-1-62798-356-3

Printed in the United States of America
First Edition
January 2014

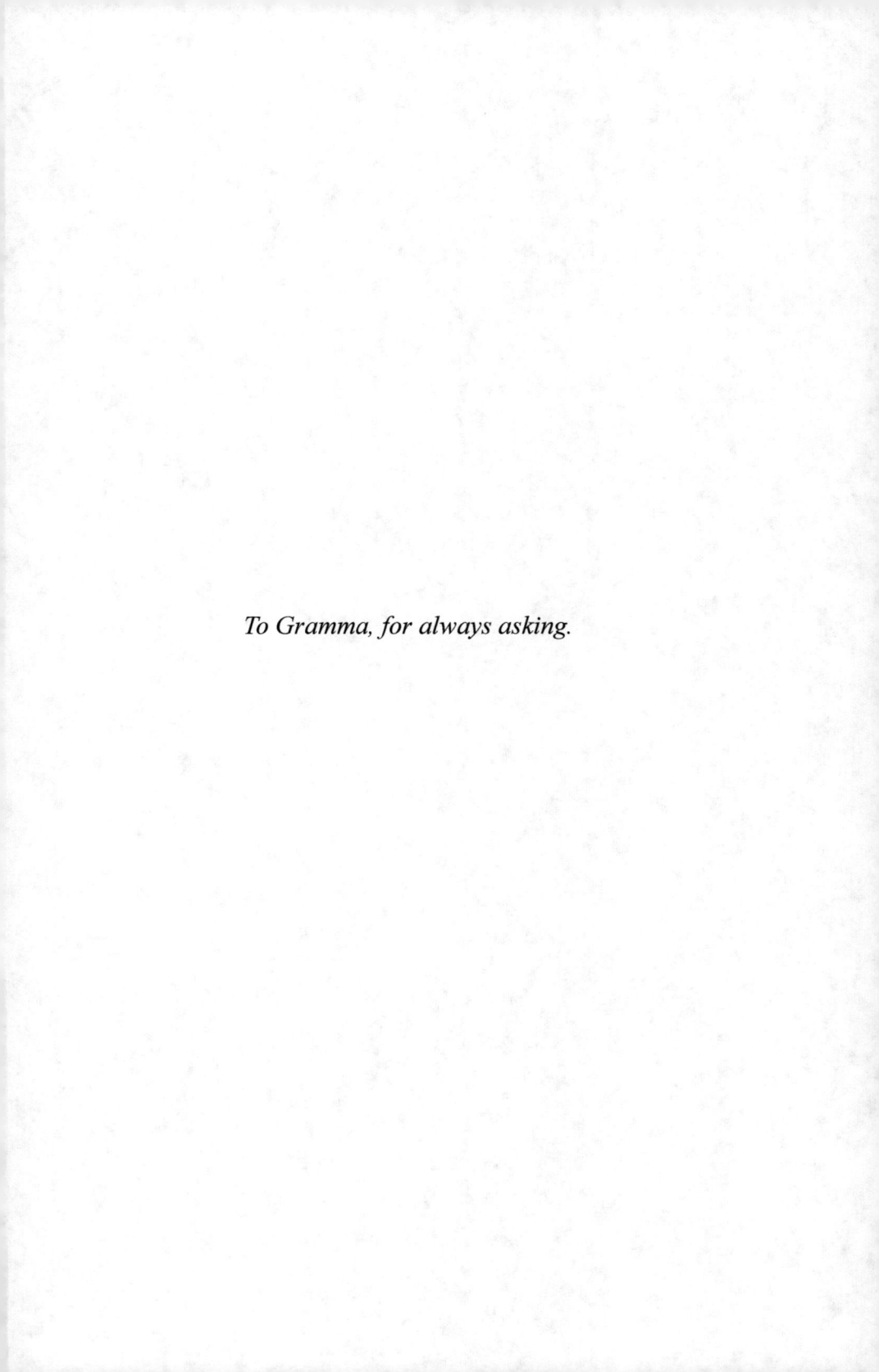

To Gramma, for always asking.

My name is Joey Mantello.
I am nineteen years old.
I am a sex slave.
I belong only to my Master, Gabriel.
I would have it no other way.

One

I COULDN'T help the silly grin from curling over my lips as Aunt Hanny stood in the hallway, her arms folded over her ample bosom. Her expression was entirely serious, and her stance let me know I wasn't going anywhere until I gave her what she wanted.

I beamed and dashed forward, scooping her up in a big, suffocating hug. "As of an hour ago, I'm officially a student at the most prestigious literary college in the state!"

I heard her gasp in delight, and thin yet strong arms wrapped around me. We danced for a few moments before she finally found the breath to say, "I knew you could do it!"

I set her down. "I can't believe it! I mean, I know I was accepted a couple weeks ago, but knowing that I'll be in the system by tomorrow afternoon makes it seem all the more real!"

She cupped my face in between her palms, her eyes misting up. "I'm so proud of you!"

I smiled shyly and let her know how much I cherished her praise. In her midfifties, she was still a very beautiful woman. She had great skin, which I was happy to have gotten from her side of the family. She was light of hair—wheat blonde streaked with gray—and I had both my mom and aunt's sparkling blue eyes. She was a little short, but her immensely cheerful attitude made up for her lack of stature. Luckily, I'd gotten my father's height—so I have been told, anyway, as I've never actually met the guy—although my teenage years left me looking like a toothpick. But this past year, I had started putting on weight and had discovered muscles I didn't even know existed.

She growled with enthusiasm and kissed me on the cheek. "I'm going to make you a hell of a dinner tonight! Mexican, your favorite!"

She was already making her way to the kitchen when I said, "I still have a lot to do. Although the scholarship will pay for tuition, it will be up to me to cover book expenses and supplies I'll need."

"You were right, you know!" she said over her shoulder as she dug out some pans.

"Huh? About what?" I asked, holding back the desire to run up to my room. I wanted to check my e-mail. I was expecting something very important. I had been running a little late this morning and hadn't had time to boot up my sluggish computer to see if I had gotten a response.

"About taking those months off. Guess that job will pay for your books and anything you might need in advance," she said.

Aunt Hanny had been adamant I go straight to college after graduating from high school, but the scholarship was good for a few years, and I had taken the three semesters off, concentrating on a low-paying job. This way I had been able to save some money. I had also insisted I at least pay for the cable bill, which she had grudgingly accepted after much nagging from me. I had told her it would make me feel like a man if I could at least cover that much. Of course, what I didn't tell her was that I also needed some alone time—time away from school and bastard bullies.

High school had been rough. Not in the academic sense, as I had aced all my classes, but kids were downright mean. Cruel. After four years of playing the punching bag, I needed a little breathing room. I knew college would be different, but I was dreading that there might be one or two "grown" bullies. I had never been one to fit in and was terrified the curse would follow me.

"Well, I'll have the money to get me started, at least. Books are ridiculously expensive, and I might have enough left over to afford a decent notebook. Do you need any help?" I asked reluctantly. Of course I wanted to help her, but I wanted to go to my room more.

She made a phish-posh noise and brushed me off. "This is for you."

I smiled and felt myself drifting toward the stairs.

"Go on, go do what you want. Dinner won't be ready for at least an hour and a half," she said distractedly, her nose in the fridge.

I let go of the breath I'd been holding, relief and excitement coursing through my veins. I yelled an "I love you" and beat feet up the stairs. I closed the door behind me and booted up my ancient desktop. I kicked off my shoes and tried to relax as the outdated piece of junk took its sweet time loading all the programs. God, I couldn't imagine what having one of those swift, new little notebooks might be like. It would be nice for sure. Aunt Hanny and I had never had a lot of money, but we had made do comfortably. After all the bills were paid, including a cheap cell phone plan, we usually had enough to go see a monthly movie or have a good dinner at a nice restaurant, so life was good.

I opened the browser and waited for it to pop up. Finally! I quickly accessed my e-mail and leaned forward, looking for a familiar e-mail address. I scrolled through all the spam, ignoring the "naughty farm girls" and "make your penis larger!" ads. I couldn't help the squeak that came from my lips when I found what I was looking for. My heart was beating hard as I read the message… twice… three times.

Dear Joey,

I like what I've read and seen so far. You interest me immensely. We should speak. If you are interested in discussing a possible contract then please give me a

call at (312) 890-9011. If you reach my voice mail,
please leave a message.

Gabriel Mason

P.S. I cannot stress how anxious I am to hear
from you. Please let me know either way.

I couldn't breathe. I was bug-eyed as I whispered the words to myself, making sure I was reading them correctly. Yes! This was what I had been waiting for after three days of silence. I dug my cell phone out of my pocket and flipped it open. With my thumb hovering over the first digit, I paused. I bit my lip as I looked at the bedroom door. I heard my aunt growl and yell something at our cat, Mischief, who had a habit of tripping you if you weren't careful. Now wasn't the time to get into a deep discussion. With dinner on the stove and Aunt Hanny lit up from all the excitement, interruption was inevitable.

It took a lot of strength to stuff my phone back into my pocket.

I sighed, whipping the mouse back and forth over the words. God, I could feel the electricity running under my skin, stirring me up. *Relax. It won't be long.* I just had to get through dinner and watch some TV with Hanny. She usually went to bed early. Then I'd have all night to talk to him.

Yeah, I could do that. It would be hard, but I could do it. Trying to keep sane, I put some music on, choosing VAST's first album—they were one of my favorite bands. I turned the stereo down until the music was a soft hum and sat back in my chair. Reading the e-mail over and over wasn't going to help. It was just going to get me more excited.

I ran my hand through my hair in boredom. It was starting to get a little long, the plain brown locks nearly reaching my eyes. I quickly typed in the web address I'd make sure to delete from my browsing history and signed in using my credentials. I scrolled through the new offers of interest, deleted them, and searched for a familiar name. I grinned ear to ear as I clicked the name, bringing up Gabriel Mason's profile.

The picture was sterile, a man sitting in an expensive leather chair, lounging. The background was that of a private office with the silhouette of downtown Chicago behind him. The man sitting in the chair was anything but plain. He was relaxed, like the world could be falling apart and he wasn't the least bit concerned. Quiet confidence oozed from his expression, his eyes looking up through dark lashes and well-manicured brows. There was a danger there that I recognized instantly, and that had been part of the reason I had shot off an e-mail to Gabriel. He had a good, strong face with a masculine jaw, and cropped black hair arranged with a carelessness that made him look younger than the thirty-six years he claimed. He had nice skin too—not too dark, not too light, but just right. He was dressed in a black dress shirt with a black-and-red pin-striped tie. In my mind, Gabriel Mason was the epitome of male perfection—successful, sexy, confident.

I felt the first hint of arousal pulse in my pants. I'd lost count how many times I'd rubbed one out to the man's picture, fantasizing that I was in that office on my knees, those sparkling gray eyes looking down at me. In my dreams, I didn't recognize Gabriel's expression but keenly felt the man's superiority. I'd wait forever if need be for Gabriel to tell me what to do. *Tell me what you want me to do. You know I'll do anything. Just tell me how to please you.*

I ran a thumb over the bulge in my jeans. My throat felt small and dry as I studied the picture until the image of Gabriel was imprinted in my mind. I wanted to pull my cock out or loosen my pants, but the texture of the denim and the constriction felt surprisingly good. Using the pad of my thumb, I traced featherlight touches over my arousal, torturing myself with pleasure.

"Joey, hon?" Aunt Hanny's voice called, followed by a knock at the door.

I snapped out of my trance and hit the off button on the screen. Clearing my throat, I said, "Come in."

Hanny's head peeked in, her smile wide. She was always good at giving me my privacy. "Do you want to come down and set the table? Dinner in fifteen."

My brows shot up. "So quickly?"

"Oh, were you dozing? It's nearly six." She smiled.

Wow, I must have been really caught up in my fantasies. "Yeah, sure. Can you give me a few minutes?"

"Sure thing."

When she closed my door, I sighed at my arousal, which was a tent in my pants. I tried to think of disgusting things like spiders, but that did very little to deflate the bulge in my jeans. I was monstrously aroused, and although I had suffered through all the embarrassments of male adolescence with Aunt Hanny, I didn't want to go downstairs packing a hard-on. I decided to take a quick cold shower, which helped, but was in no way a fix to my raging desire.

Just think, the sooner you go downstairs and have dinner with Hanny, the sooner she'll go to bed, and you'll be alone.

That was all the encouragement I needed.

I LOOKED at my aunt as she drooped in her chair. Dinner had been longer than expected, but delicious. She had made tacos and enchiladas, beans, rice, and even homemade salsa—all my favorites—and I'd eaten until I was stuffed. Normally, with the possibility of meeting up with Gabriel, I would be watching my caloric intake more closely—which was ridiculous, considering I could do with putting on a few pounds, but I was in too good a mood not to celebrate. Hanny had even broken out a bottle of cheap wine, and we'd toasted to my future.

After dinner, we had sat down to watch some TV, which was the normal evening routine. I had tried my best to concentrate on what was showing on the screen, but my mind was preoccupied with getting upstairs and on the phone. Finally, at half past eight, Hanny began to droop. I watched her carefully, judging her movements, her posture.

Timing it right, I stretched and yawned, saying, "Wow! I'm tired. Must have been all the excitement!"

"Oh! I think I wore myself out too. I'm going to head to bed as well," she declared, and shut off the television.

I walked her to her bedroom, kissed her cheek, then rushed to my room, closing the door softly. I made for my bathroom, brushed my teeth, and swished some mouthwash (which was dumb, it wasn't like Gabriel would be able to smell my breath through the phone). I got comfortable in a T-shirt and a pair of loose-fitting jogging pants, then plopped on my bed and relaxed. I gripped my phone, not yet ready to make the call. Just a few more minutes to make sure Hanny was asleep. I'd waited this long, I could wait a little longer.

I watched the minutes tick by, counting out the seconds. It felt like an eternity, and I realized, as I flipped open my phone, that my hesitation wasn't just from fear of being interrupted, but because I was nervous. *It's just a phone call*, I chided myself.

More time passed, my thumb hovering over the numbers I'd memorized. This was silly. I was excited. I wanted to talk to Gabriel, hear the man's voice, so why was I trembling like a five-year-old? It's not like we were face-to-face.

Finding my courage, I dialed the number and pressed the phone to my ear, my guts tumbling like a cement mixer. The first ring startled me, but when I realized that was a normal sound for someone making a phone call, I relaxed slightly. It rang a second time, and then a third… fourth…. Crap. I wondered if it was too late and he'd gone to bed. He was a businessman after all.

Before I could decide to hang up, the line clicked.

"Mason speaking." The tone was casual, if not a little bored.

I opened my mouth and… did nothing. I gulped like a fish, like an idiot. *Say something, geez!* The only thing my sluggish brain could come up with was a very raspy, "Hi."

The man on the other end of the line was silent for a moment. When he spoke, his voice shifted from quiet annoyance to dark amusement. "Joey?"

"Yes, sir," I breathed out. "It's me. I, uh, sorry I didn't call sooner. Were you sleeping or something?" I was proud that I had managed a complete sentence.

"I never sleep," he said simply. "But I'm glad you called. I was just relaxing for the evening. Long day, as usual. How was yours?"

I felt my heart jump. Gabriel had a great voice, deep and sexy, and the way he pronounced his words with eloquence excited me. I could just imagine him whispering commands into my ear. *Mm*.... "Great! I, um... I had a good day. Sorry... yours wasn't."

Gabriel chuckled, and I wasn't sure what he found funny. It was probably my sudden case of stuttering. I reminded myself that I needed to stay cool.

"You *sound* as if you've had a very good day," Gabriel remarked, and I thought he might be smiling.

"Yeah, I'm now an official student at Simone University," I boasted. It felt amazing to have achieved so much with so little.

"You've mentioned something about that in your e-mail. I'm happy for you," he said, his words making me smile like a dork. "Well, Joey.... Tell me, what are you doing this moment?"

I swallowed hard, trying to ignore the sudden erection popping up. God, I could come from just listening to his voice. I played it cool. "Nothing much, just sitting here. On my bed. Hanny made dinner for me." I silently bonked myself on the head. My words were all over the place, my thoughts jumbled. I must have sounded like an idiot.

"Hanny?" Gabriel asked.

"My aunt. I, uh... live with her," I said, hoping I didn't sound like a squatter. I was nineteen, I needed to find my own place soon, but money was tight. "It's just been us for a long time and... I guess I don't want to leave her alone." Why would he care about my home life?

"It's good that you have someone to share your accomplishments with," he said simply. "And now it's late, and you're on the phone with me."

His tone was completely suggestive, the dark curl like a physical tug on my cock. I took a deep breath and closed my eyes. "Yeah. I wanted to call earlier, but I figured with Hanny in bed... more privacy."

"Wise decision," Gabriel whispered. "Now tell me what drew you to my profile. I'm curious to know why you chose me out of the thousands of others."

I took a moment to think and decided on simple truth. "Your eyes."

Gabriel made a sound of acknowledgment. "What about them?"

I ran my hand down my abdomen, the cloth against my skin seeming rough. I let my breath go slowly. "You look like you could make someone shake in their shoes from just a single look."

"Hm... you like dangerous men, Joey?" he purred.

I forced a lump down my throat, letting my hand wander farther south. "I don't know. I just know that I like what I saw. Honestly, I didn't think I'd get a response."

"And why is that?" Gabriel asked, sounding genuinely interested.

"I don't know... the picture I put up made me look like a dork," I admitted. When Gabriel didn't respond, I said, "I mean... I had to take it myself, and that's kind of hard to do. Not to mention my camera is crap. I got it from a resale shop...." I really needed to shut up.

Gabriel was silent for a few moments, and I believed I'd just blown my chance. Why would this sexy, powerful man be interested in a kid like me?

"It was not your picture that interested me. You are a very handsome young man, Joey, but that was not the reason I responded to your e-mail."

"Oh." I gaped. I wanted to ask what the reason was, but my mind went blank.

"Can I ask you a question?" Gabriel said.

Something did a somersault in my stomach. "Yes, sir."

"Are you really nineteen?" he asked seriously.

"Yes… I… yes, sir."

Gabriel chuckled. "You don't sound too sure."

I cleared my throat. "Sorry, your question just caught me off guard."

"Reason I ask is because a lot of men on *Bindfind* tend to lie about their age because they think all us dirty old men want barely legal teenagers. Not true at all," he explained matter-of-factly, but I was sure there was a hint of frustration there. "Truth be told, I generally don't go for men of your age or inexperience."

My heart dropped. "Oh."

"However, in this case, I made an exception," he said, his tone bordering on amusement. "Your maturity and witty sense of humor intrigued me. So, here we are."

I heard the smile in his voice, and I couldn't help my own from creeping onto my face. "That's… good. I'm glad you did."

Silence courted us for a few moments, and I thought I heard a cricket. Our e-mail exchanges had been fairly benign, simple hi-what-are-you-up-to with a little mix of shared opinions on recent news events, but I was glad he viewed me as mature—I was afraid I'd come off as a horny little boy.

Gabriel let out a soft breath. "If you are indeed interested in pursuing a contract, then I think we should meet. Have dinner with me tomorrow."

It wasn't a question, but an order. My cock jumped in my pants. I forced myself to relax, thrilled that Gabriel was still interested in me. "That sounds great, sir." Deep down, though, I was shaking at the thought of meeting this man.

"You are free tomorrow, correct?" he inquired, his tone dark.

"Yes, sir," I said. I didn't start college for another four weeks, and I'd quit my job, so I had a lot of free time. If I were lucky, I would get to spend it with him.

"Do you have a car?" Gabriel asked, something shuffling in the distance.

I blushed, embarrassed. "No, sir."

"Hm, can you bus it to the Midway transportation depot? I can pick you up from there. You said you lived on the south side, and that would be the closest to you," he said.

"That's perfect. There is a bus stop right in front of my house." Excitement coursed through me, making my insides bounce.

"Say… six o'clock. That should give us enough time to talk. I will be driving a black Camaro. You already know what I look like."

"Yes, sir, that's good." Oh my God, was this really happening?

"Then it's done. Joey, if for whatever reason you decide you don't want to do this, I would ask that you have the courtesy to at least let me know," he said, and I could hear the warning in his tone. "I would not be very happy to travel so far south of the city for nothing."

"Yes, of course, sir." There was no way short of the end of the world I was going to miss this. I might be nervous as heck, but I wanted it so bad, it was all I ever thought about lately. I had quickly gone from the fantasizing-during-masturbation phase to wanting to experience it with another human being.

"Good," he said on an expulsion of breath. "Do you have somewhere you have to be in the morning, or do you have some more time to talk with me?"

"No, sir. I can talk." Like I was getting off the phone with Gabriel? Pfft.

"Wonderful." His tone seemed to lighten a bit, as if he enjoyed talking to me.

I smiled, glad I could talk with him a little longer.

11

"Tell me, when did you begin to take an interest in the lifestyle?" he asked. "You are incredibly young, if indeed you are being truthful."

"I am, I promise," I confirmed. "I... I've always thought about it, about things...." Oh boy, how did I explain it?

"How old were you when you first had these thoughts?" he inquired.

"Ah, I think maybe twelve or thirteen. I would tie—" I cut myself off, my cheeks heating.

"You sound very nervous, Joey. Do you think it would be any easier discussing this face-to-face? Are you sure you're ready?" the man inquired, his tone level, as if he were trying to be understanding.

"Absolutely. I—I can't explain it, but I know what I want." I had known for a very long time. "I would tie my hands behind my back with rubber bands and, ah, rub against my pillow."

I cleared my throat, feeling a little embarrassed at the admission. Gabriel was quiet for several moments, and I thought that maybe he was waiting for me to speak more, but....

"Do you still do this?" he inquired.

"Yes."

"Would you tell me about it, Joey?" Gabriel purred, his voice so very low and dark. "In detail, so I can picture it."

My mouth fell open, and my cock jerked in my pants. I had never imagined our conversation would go in this direction so quickly. "I... yes... sir. They are the big rubber bands, the kind you could fit two hands in."

"Yes, I know what you are referring to. Please, continue on," Gabriel said, but I could hear the quiet demand in his voice, and that excited me even more.

I took a deep breath and let it out to steady myself. "I would put the pillow in the middle of the bed, and I would lie on my side.

Then I would secure my hands behind my back and grind against the pillow until I, uh, came."

Gabriel chuckled, and it went right to my cock. "Details, Joey. I want details."

Oh. I thought I had been detailed, but....

"I have an idea. Are you willing to play along?" he whispered.

"Yes, sir," I answered before I could think.

"If you are not naked, then get that way now," he commanded, his tone coming through the phone.

I swallowed so hard it hurt. "Yes... sir. I'll, uh... be right back."

"Quickly, Joey."

I put my cell phone down and lifted my hips as I pulled my pants off. My cock was hard and heavy, and the cool air hitting it was startling. I discarded my pants on the floor, my shirt quickly following.

I picked up the phone. "I'm here."

"Arrange yourself as you usually do. Will you be able to hold the phone with your shoulder?"

"Ah, yes, sir... one second."

I set the phone down again and rearranged everything, retrieving my rubber bands from the bedside table and the pillow I kept tucked between the bed and the wall. My heart was banging hard, and I could barely breathe, but I managed to get comfortable on my side with the pillow pressing against my hips. I pressed the cell against my ear, holding it secure with my shoulder.

"I'm back," I said.

"Are you in position?" Gabriel asked, his tone strained.

"Yes, sir."

"Tell me what the pillow feels like against your cock. Are you hard, Joey?"

God, the way Gabriel purred my name—it was so erotic, and the undertone of danger aroused me. I cleared my throat. "I've been hard since I got home and read your e-mail."

Gabriel chuckled, the sound going right to my dick. "Honest. That's good. Now tell me what it feels like."

I licked my lips and positioned my cock so that it was flush against the pillow, halfway under me. "Scratchy, yet soft and cool. It's a duck-feather pillow, and sometimes the little quills stick through."

"Are you circumcised?" he inquired.

"Yes, sir," I said.

"Good," Gabriel practically growled. "Now secure your hands behind your back and tell me when you are done."

"Yes, sir." I took the three rubber bands and wrapped them around my left wrist, then put my hands behind my back. I had to wiggle my right hand through, and when I got it in, the twisting rubber snapped at my skin and I hissed. "I got it."

"Good boy. Can't move?" he inquired.

"No, sir. When I am done, I just slide my arms around my legs... if that makes any sense."

"I understand what you are saying. Now listen and listen closely, Joey. I want you to do as I tell you. Do you understand?" he said, his voice hardly more than a growl.

The authority made my cock throb, and I sputtered a "Yes, sir."

"Start moving against the pillow, slowly," he ordered.

I drew my hips back and thrust forward, and the pleasure was instantaneous, the raspy fabric exciting the head of my cock. My breath quickly hitched, and I had to bite my lip to keep from moaning.

"Are you holding back on me, Joey?" Gabriel demanded. "Let me hear you. Tell me what it feels like."

I gasped, both from the sound of Gabriel's voice and the sensation of the pillow. "So good, sir. Feels almost like sandpaper against the underside of my cock."

"How long does it usually take you to achieve orgasm this way?"

"Maybe… two or three minutes… sir," I panted as tension grew in my balls. The sound of this amazing man's voice had increased the pleasure tenfold.

"Do not come unless I tell you to, Joey."

"Yes, sir," I muttered, then gasped as one of the quills bit at my cock.

"What happened?" Gabriel inquired, but I had a feeling he already knew.

"One of the quills."

"Don't stop. Keep rubbing up against it."

"Yes, sir," I said and continued to hump the pillow. When that quill scraped a sensitive area, I moaned.

"That's it. Good boy, let me hear you."

Oh God, even though those little sharp quills stung, it felt too good to stop. Besides, Gabriel had told me to keep going, and the praise in his tone made me smile. I tried to imagine him standing over me, barking orders, maybe spanking me a little when I hesitated.

"I'm so close…," I groaned, trying to keep myself from rocking against the pillow like a maniac.

"Stop," Gabriel ordered.

I moaned in protest but obeyed, the orgasm so close to the surface. I balled my fists, the rubber bands biting into my skin.

After a few moments, Gabriel commanded, "Continue."

I whispered a "Yes, sir" and started thrusting against the pillow again, trying to stick to a slow, steady rhythm, but it was hard, the intense curl in my balls demanding I come. A moan bubbled up from my throat. I knew what was coming.

"Stop," he ordered.

I groaned, pulling my hips back, nearly shooting my load.

"Close that time?" he inquired.

"Yes, sir, but I stopped," I murmured.

"You ever hold your orgasm, Joey?"

"No, sir, not really."

The man tsked. "The journey is all the fun."

I smiled at the teasing in his voice. My cock had started to throb incessantly, my balls getting tight. Eventually, Gabriel told me to start again, and I did, the rasping against the sensitive head of my dick teasing the orgasm out.

"You want to come, Joey?" Gabriel purred.

"Yes, please," I whimpered.

"Beg me," he growled.

I gasped at the command and pleasure. "Please, sir... let me come. I've been hard all day thinking about you... I need to come so bad. I really need it."

"I bet you do," he teased in that wolfish voice. "Come for me, Joey, and let me hear you."

I thrust hard against the pillow and gasped as the quill scraped against me, but I didn't stop rocking. When I exploded, I just let go... groaning my pleasure into the phone, giving Gabriel what he had demanded.

"That's it. Good boy," he said softly.

My cries eventually wound down to contented moans, and a big, dumb smile spread over my face.

"Good?"

"Yes, sir... thank you," I mumbled.

Gabriel chuckled. "It's late, and I have work in the morning. Remember what I said. If you decide this isn't for you, let me know."

"I will, sir," I said, not wanting to get off the phone.

"Get some sleep, Joey."

"Good night."

I heard the phone click and turned onto my back, slipping my hands through my legs. I undid the rubber bands, the skin around my wrists red, then cleaned up as best I could. My pillow was covered in spunk, so I simply stuck it back in between the bed and the wall, deciding I'd wash it later. All I wanted to do right now was relax and think about what had just happened.

I lay on my back and examined my semihard cock. The head was flushed, and the underside where the quill had scraped at me felt a little sore. I liked it. I had contemplated going for round two but felt the urge to sleep hit me quickly. Besides, I had a big day ahead of me tomorrow, and I could use all the rest I could get. I was aware that my transition into the world of BDSM would be nothing short of mind-blowing.

Gabriel Mason. I let his name roll off my tongue. What a solid, strong name. God, I couldn't wait until tomorrow night.

Two

I'D GOTTEN up early the next morning, had breakfast, then taken a long, hot bath, scrubbing my body well in preparation for my meeting with Gabriel. I clipped my nails and plucked a stray hair from my brow, which hurt, and even trimmed my pubes. Honestly, I had no idea what to expect tonight. Gabriel had said talk, but what about after?

I sighed. It was only 2:00 p.m. I planned to leave at four, just in case traffic was heavy, but that seemed like such a long way away. My stomach turned, and it was not due to skipping lunch, but nerves. Of course I was freaking out. Was I having reservations? Nope.

I dragged my feet back up to my room and, for the third time today, debated about what I would wear. Gabriel was a businessman, so the restaurant he had chosen was probably high-end, which meant no T-shirts and jeans. I had tried on my nicest dress shirt and slacks but had turned out looking like a dweeb on school-picture day. That just wasn't going to work. I wanted to project the image of a man, not a boy.

What would he like? I had no idea.

I riffled through my dresser and found a gray cashmere sweater I had bought at the thrift store for five bucks. The tag had been cut off, but it looked expensive. I threw it over my head, happy to find that it fit perfectly—not too tight, not too loose. Now… what about pants?

I snapped my fingers. I dug through my closet and found a fairly new pair of tan khakis. I slipped into them and admired myself in the mirror for a good twenty minutes. Yeah, I thought, this would work. I actually looked like a college student—relaxed, comfortable, yet classy. I hoped Gabriel would approve.

By the time four o'clock came around, I was a mess, both dreading and looking forward to the meeting. I had told Hanny earlier I was going to a seminar for new students that the college was holding this evening and wouldn't be home until late. She wished me good luck with a kiss on the cheek and told me how nice I looked. I hoped she wasn't just being a doting auntie. I knew I had a severe lack of self-confidence, thanks to the schoolyard bullies.

As I waited for the bus to arrive, I pulled in the cool spring air, the scent of new flowers heavy. My stomach was a wreck. Luckily, I hadn't eaten anything. Then again, that could be why. I could do this. All new things were scary at first, and besides, Gabriel said we'd just talk. I thought that was a good idea. I'd never really put words to my deepest secrets before, and talking to someone of like mind might help.

The bus ride was uneventful, but each block closer to the transportation depot made me shiver from nervous excitement. I rested my head against the window and closed my eyes, concentrating on breathing. My biggest fear was that he wouldn't like me, physically or otherwise. I needed to calm down, though. All the nerves were liable to make me clumsy, and the last thing I wanted to do was trip in front of Gabriel Mason.

We finally turned in to the depot, and my eyes instantly scanned for a black Camaro, but it was only a quarter after five—I still had forty-five minutes. After exiting the bus, I took a seat on a stone flowerbed by the pickup horseshoe and stuck the buds of my outdated CD player into my ears. As the music jammed, I managed to calm down and closed my eyes as I absorbed the lyrics. Before I knew it, it was ten to six, and I stuffed my belongings back into my backpack.

Well… it was time, I told myself, and stood up. Several cars turned in, picked up commuters and schoolkids, then rolled away. No Camaro yet. It wasn't until quarter after that I checked my phone, and my insides fell. Maybe he couldn't make it? Did I miss an e-mail or a phone call?

Just as I started to scroll though my phone for missed calls, a roar caught my attention and a sleek black car pulled in. Oh God… it was him. I just knew it. The windows were lightly tinted, but I could see the form of a man sitting at the wheel. I forced myself to breathe as the car rolled up. My belly started churning again, and I swallowed something big. I took a deep breath to try and steady myself, but it did very little to help.

The Camaro came to a stop, and I saw the car door open. The air quickly heated and a hot summer breeze rushed in at me, making me sweat—or it could have been the man exiting the car.

He was dressed in business attire: a black dress shirt and slacks with a leather jacket thrown over his strong shoulders. And he was so very tall. I was a healthy six feet, but he looked as if he towered several inches over me… and those shades hid dangerous eyes. He was so handsome, even more so in person. He had a sort of dangerous aura about him, as if he were a highly trained bodyguard rather than a businessman. It aroused me and intimidated me in one go.

His lips quirked up. "Joey?"

My eyes widened and my cock jerked at the sound of that deep, rich voice calling my name. I opened my mouth to try and speak. "I… hi… Sir—Gab… I?"

My cheeks flushed from embarrassment. What was wrong with me that I couldn't even speak?

That smile lifted just a little more, and he nodded to his car. "Come sit down before you fall down."

All the blood went to my face, and I managed to peel my feet from the ground. He tracked me as I neared, those shades hiding a predator's gaze, I didn't doubt. I bit my lip as I opened the door and slipped in. Gabriel Mason came to join me, closing the door behind him. I suddenly felt caged with a wild animal—but I liked it. I watched, stunned, as he propped an elbow on the door and turned to look at me. His lips moved slightly, and I thought he might be talking to me, but my brain was slogging along, completely destroyed by this man.

"Joey?"

"Hm?" I managed.

"You can put your bag in the backseat," he reiterated.

Oh, right. I managed to do it with shaky hands, and I knew without looking that intense stare was still directed at me. Did he like what he saw?

"You are right," he said. "Your profile picture makes you look like a dork."

My attention shot to him. Oh God, did that mean he…?

Those cool shades were whipped off, and his eyes did a once-over on me, his tongue running across his bottom lip. His eyes were like bottled lightning, so light gray they were nearly silver. His gaze finally settled on me, and I thought I'd be burned alive.

"You are much more handsome in person."

My heart and cock thumped in unison. "T-thank you, sir."

"Give me your hand," he said, his voice going a little dark.

Before I could think, I offered him my left hand. He took it, turning my palm up. His skin was so warm and a little rough, but he was touching me. He started circling my palm with a finger, the sensation pleasant if not a little ticklish.

"Close your eyes," he said, his concentration on what he was doing.

I obeyed and focused on Gabriel's touch and how nice it felt. He stopped that swirling motion, then pinched the flesh between my thumb and forefinger. I wasn't sure what he was doing, but—I moaned softly as I relaxed, the shivers easing, the washing machine in my belly turned on low until I managed to breathe evenly. When he took his hand away, I opened my eyes to look at him.

"Better?"

I nodded. "Thank you."

"Good." He winked playfully. "I thought you were going to pass out there for a moment."

I blushed but didn't say anything.

"It's nice to finally meet you, Joey." He smiled softly.

"You too, sir," I said, managing only a clumsy grin, but he seemed delighted by my awkwardness.

"Are you ready?" Gabriel asked, his tone a wicked curl, as if he had evil plans in store for me.

"Very much, yes." I had waited for this for a long time, and I hoped he was the one to show me to the door that housed all my desires.

He chuckled. "You might want to close the door. I don't want you falling out of the car."

I looked to my side and gasped, realizing that the passenger door was still open. As I closed it, I didn't think it was possible to blush more than I already was. I followed Gabriel's example, fastening the seat belt and relaxing back against the seat. The car jerked slightly, the engine roaring. Gabriel was not loose with the pedal.

He came off as a very confident man, one in control of his life and the people around him, and his driving was no different. Though he weaved in and out, bypassed slower vehicles without hesitation, he was very cautious, as if he owned the road.

As we headed for the expressway, I felt the need to break the silence. "Where are we going?"

"A place called Olympus. Cliché name, amazing food. The atmosphere is lovely as well," he said, concentrating on the road.

"Is it in Greek Town?" I inquired.

"A little north, but close."

I nodded, my throat dry. I wasn't sure if I could eat anything. I was freaking out.

"How was your day, Joey?" Gabriel asked.

I looked at the man next to me, his eyes sparkling in the dusk light. He had a strong jaw, perfectly cut. Remembering he'd asked a question, I said, "Good. I didn't do much. I have a few weeks off before classes start, so I'm just kind of enjoying my time off."

"That's good. I hardly ever get more than the weekend off, and even then I'm doing work at home," he said simply, as if it were the norm.

"What do you do, again?"

"Financial manager for one the largest banking firms in America. We have several high-profile investors living in the area, so the firm asked me to make Chicago my permanent place of residence so I could personally meet with them when the time calls for it," he said, cocking the wheel to the left. We zoomed into the fast lane and bypassed cars as if they were static. "Keeps me busy, anyhow. If I'm lucky, I'll have something else to keep me occupied."

I didn't miss the undertone in those words, and my cock woke up to the thought. There were so many more things I wanted to ask, but I couldn't think right now, much less speak. I so wanted to keep Gabriel busy.

"What choice of career have you decided on?" Gabriel asked.

I bit my lip. "Ah, I'm not exactly sure. I was thinking journalism, but I have a year to decide. Right now I'm just covering the literary basics."

"You like to write?" he inquired.

"Yes, sir, very much." I nodded.

"That's good." He grinned, those lips rising.

Feeling suddenly light, I went on. "I had a few poems published in high school as part of a program. I didn't make any money off it, though, but it was fun. Where the jocks had their sports bragging rights, I sort of had my literary fame…. Anyway."

Gabriel chuckled but didn't say anything. I bit my lip and returned my attention to the road. Maybe I shouldn't say too much. I didn't want to come off as immature, seeing as my only life experiences were from high school.

"I was notorious in high school," Gabriel started, and I snapped my attention to him.

When he didn't go on, I asked, "Were you a football hero? Basketball, maybe?"

Gabriel glanced at me, his expression smug amusement. "More like a goth monstrosity."

I felt my jaw slacken. "Really?"

He shrugged as if he didn't particularly find it amusing.

I couldn't help but mumble, "I bet you scared the shit out of everyone."

Gabriel snickered evilly. I could just imagine this man with long black hair, dressing in black leather and chains, those electric eyes striking fear into everyone. It was a nice picture. I would have been his friend any day. If there was one thing I'd learned from high school, the outsiders were the nicest of people, and it was the popular kids you had to watch out for. My only friends had been the fat kids and the nerds and the skaters. They were all really good peeps. The small goth crew at the high school had been the same way. They tended to freak everyone out, but if you talked to them just a little, they were fairly accepting.

"So, no sports for you? I mean, not even basketball? You're pretty tall," I inquired.

"Nah, bad knee. What about you?"

"Oh, I was on the track team for a few years. I wasn't very good, though it kept me in shape." I blushed.

"Well, sports are overrated." I got the feeling he was trying to make me feel better, but I didn't question it.

We didn't say anything else the rest of the drive. I didn't go downtown much, and all the people and lights and cars grabbed my attention. We parked in a five-story garage, Gabriel selecting the most expensive option, which consisted of a valet. The parking fees and dinner were probably going to cost as much as I made in a week at my part-time job. I had brought some money with me, not knowing what to expect. Would it be out of place to offer to pay for anything? Gabriel seemed like the kind of man to take care of everything. I didn't want to offend him.

My nerves returned as we exited the car.

The walk over to the restaurant was a short one, and as we neared, I could hear soft foreign music playing and the hum of dozens of people talking. There were flowerpots all over with real spring flowers in them, and statues of Greek gods and goddesses. Gabriel led me in and walked up to the hostess. I couldn't keep my eyes from dropping to his ass, which was, unfortunately, covered by his jacket.

"Reservation for Gabriel Mason," he said, his tone even but stern, as if he demanded top-notch service.

"Ah, yes... you reserved five tables. Will the rest of your guests be arriving shortly?"

"No, it will just be us."

"Ah, okay.... Right this way, Mr. Mason." The woman smiled awkwardly and led us into a small dining area away from most of the crowd.

Five tables? Okay, so the dinner alone was probably going to cost two weeks of my wages. I imagined a restaurant of this caliber charged a small fee to reserve so many tables.

The lights were low, and the booth she showed us to was in a quiet corner. I took my seat, watching as Gabriel shrugged out of his leather jacket, his shoulders rolling. He sat down as the hostess set the menus on the table.

Our waitress introduced herself and asked, "Any wine this evening, sirs?"

"I'll have your best white zinfandel," Gabriel said.

The waitress turned to regard me. I blushed, hating that legally I couldn't drink. "Just water, please."

"Very well," she said and left.

I picked up the menu and glanced at the offerings. Everything sounded mouthwatering, but I wasn't sure I could eat. I could feel Gabriel's eyes on me, and I wondered what he was thinking.

"Allow me to order for you," he said, and though it was posed as a polite request, I recognized a command there.

I swallowed hard and nodded.

The waitress quickly returned. I watched as she set up the ice bucket and popped the cork. I'd never seen it done before, not in person, anyway, so it was fascinating to me. She poured a small amount into a wineglass, and Gabriel accepted it. He took a moment to swirl it around, then sipped, smacking his lips. He nodded, apparently pleased with the flavor.

"I will return in a few moments to take your orders."

"Take your time," Gabriel said. When she was gone, those silver eyes fell on me. "How are you doing? Feel a little dizzy?"

I blushed and looked down. "Sorry. This... is all new to me."

"I know," he said and took another sip of wine.

I watched as he snapped his napkin, then wiped the glass where he had drunk. He offered it to me, and all I could do was blink.

"Don't tell me you and your friends haven't sneaked a few six-packs before," he said, his brow arching.

I smiled meekly and accepted the glass. No, I'd never had any close friends to share in said adventures with, but Aunt Hanny did offer me a little wine on special occasions such as New Year's Eve. "I've never had zinfandel before."

I took a tiny sip... and another, and found the flavor to be nice, pleasant, and not pungent like the can of beer I had stolen from the fridge. I offered the glass back to him, and he took it, our fingers brushing gently. I managed to speak. "It's not bad."

He didn't respond but proceeded to pierce me with those intense eyes, as if he were studying me or expecting me to say something. I looked away.

"Tell me about you. Have you lived in Chicago all your life?" he inquired, his tone curious.

"Yes, sir," I said. "Though I was born in the burbs. You?"

He shrugged. "Most of my childhood years were spent in southern Wisconsin. Nothing interesting there. So, it's just you and your aunt?"

I smiled. "My mother died when I was a baby, so Aunt Hanny took me in and raised me as her own. I never knew my father, but we've done great, at least I like to think so."

"That's good," he said, his tone deepening. "Sometimes it's better not knowing who your father is."

I wasn't sure what that meant, but I got the feeling he was in a similar position. Biting my lip, I looked away. I had always wondered who my father was, his name, what he looked like, but my mother seemed not to have known either. At least that was the impression Aunt Hanny gave me when I asked questions about Mom.

"Joey."

God, how he said my name…. All I could think about was the way he had ordered me to orgasm last night. He'd probably done it many times to many different men, driving them wild with just his voice. "Yes, sir?"

When I looked at him, his lips were curled slightly, as if he was enjoying my awkwardness.

"Is there anything you might like to ask me?" he inquired. "Now is the time."

So many things, I thought. But where did I begin? I frowned. "It's somewhat personal."

"If things go where I hope they do, it's going to get very personal," he said on a growl, as if he were savoring the thought.

27

Oh God, this man was going to kill me, really. I took a deep breath. "I was just curious…. I mean, you've obviously been doing… *this* for a long time, and, ah, how come you don't…. um, have anyone?"

Gabriel seemed to reflect on my jumble of words for a moment before answering. "My last boy left me a year ago."

"Oh." I bit my lip. Something dark entered the man's eyes, a shine, or perhaps it was just the low light catching. "Was he young like me? Did he go off to college or something?"

Gabriel took a sip of his wine. "No, he died."

I looked down, feeling bad for pressing the point. "I'm sorry."

Gabriel shrugged. "These things happen. And as I told you before, I don't usually take interest in such tender meat."

My mouth was suddenly parched, and I took a drink of my water.

"So, what about you, Joey? Tell me more about what you want," he asked, leaning in as if he were truly interested in my thoughts.

The waitress returned, and Gabriel seemed mildly annoyed with her presence, but he started naming food. He ordered Greek chicken and potatoes for the both of us, which sounded quite yummy to me—if I could manage to actually eat anything.

When she was gone, Gabriel said, "I'm still waiting for an answer."

I took another drink of water. "I, ah… I want…." I knew what I wanted; it was just hard to put it into words.

Gabriel leaned back against the booth and sighed. "If you cannot even put a name to it, then how can you be sure it is what you want?"

I looked away, not sure how to answer that question. "Maybe I don't have a name."

"Then tell me what it is you dream about late at night. Tell me what you think about when you play with yourself, Joey," Gabriel said, his eyes lighting up the room. "Tell me about those deep, dark fantasies that you think you could never ever tell anyone because they couldn't possibly understand."

I was sure I gasped, the room suddenly hot and stuffy. I looked around, unsure, scared that anyone might hear.

Gabriel snapped his fingers to get my attention. "There is no one in earshot. I made sure of it."

It calmed me a little that he had gone through all the trouble to provide a peaceful environment where we could relax and talk with little interruption… and I wasn't doing much talking, was I? I took a deep breath and plucked a random fantasy from my mind.

"I see this man standing over me. I'm on my knees. He makes me bathe his thighs with my tongue…." My voice was way too raspy, so I took another drink. "Then he makes me move up and start working on his… balls. And…."

"Keep talking, Joey. Tell me what else he wants you to do," Gabriel commanded. He was completely focused on me, his eyes drilling, his body reaching.

"He makes me suck him while he… ah, spanks me with… I don't know what it is, but it's small and stings, and I—" My hands were shaking as I lifted the glass to my lips. I managed to collect myself to say, "My hands are tied behind my back."

I stared at Gabriel's wineglass, unable to comprehend what I had just put into words. But if anyone could understand what I was feeling, it was this man.

"Joey, look at me," Gabriel commanded. I managed to drag my eyes to his. "It feels better, doesn't it? Saying it out loud."

I let go of the breath I hadn't realized I was holding. He was right. Even though I was nervous, I felt a lot better having been able to talk about the fantasy. I nodded, unable to keep from smiling.

The waitress returned with two salad plates and set them in front of us. I watched, transfixed, as she added a little pepper to the mix of greens upon his request. The first bite he took was a tomato, and I was astonished at the way his jaw moved.

"Eat your salad, Joey," he said. "You'll get your dessert later."

I snapped out of it and blushed, my cock hardening. Honestly, I had been in a state of semiarousal all evening, but Gabriel got me more and more excited with only a few words. I managed to eat most of it, avoiding the olives, more interested in watching Gabriel eat. He was elegant, as if he'd come from an old, rich family where dinner manners were an important part of life.

"You doing okay?" he inquired, filling his wineglass.

"Yes, sir."

"Tell me more," he ordered.

I wet my throat with some water. The fantasy I had admitted to had been one of the tamer ones, and I wasn't sure how much deeper I was willing to go. As I hesitated, Gabriel seemed to be annoyed with my reluctance, and I told myself this might be my only opportunity to explore what I so badly wanted.

"I... the man makes me crawl around, getting things for him, using my back to hold his wineglass." My gaze was drawn to Gabriel's glass. I cleared my throat. "And... he puts things in me."

I saw the smile twitch on Gabriel's lips, but I was still shocked I had managed to admit that. But geez, what was it they said—confession was good for the soul? I suddenly felt confidence rise in me. "Sometimes I see myself like this, and so much time has passed. He finally comes home from somewhere, and I help him undress, relax... then he... ah, uses me."

"Who is this man, Joey?" Gabriel asked simply, but his face looked a little tight, as if he were struggling with something.

I shrugged. "I don't know. He's more like a silhouette, if you know what I mean... a stand-in."

Gabriel nodded and took a drink from his glass, his tongue swiping across his bottom lip. "Does he make you beg, Joey? Hm? Beg to let you suck his cock? To fuck you? To let you come?"

Oh God, the words were so naughty. All I could feel was my cock pressing against my pants. My skin flushed, and my heart was throbbing in my ears. I might have moaned. I probably did.

Gabriel chuckled. "I'll take that as a yes."

The waitress arrived with the food, and I wished she would hurry up as she set the plates in front of us. I wanted to tell Gabriel more. Maybe he could tell me things. I watched blankly as he divided his meal, most of it going into the container he had requested. I turned my attention to my own. It all looked and smelled very good, but I didn't have much of an appetite. Still, it would be rude to not eat what had been ordered for me.

We ate in mostly silence, Gabriel asking if I liked the food, to which I answered yes. My favorite was the potatoes, and he agreed. When we were done, he took what was left of my meal and scraped it into a container, then set the plates aside.

As he filled his glass with a little more wine, he said, "Are you interested in telling me more?"

I smiled shyly. "Yes, actually."

He listened intently, his eyes bright with interest as I talked about my fantasies, and it wasn't long before the words just started pouring out of my mouth. He made it so easy to talk about it, partly because I knew he had probably made men do such things for him, but he was also a good listener, encouraging me when I wasn't sure how to broach a certain subject.

I wasn't sure how long we'd talked, but my mouth had gone dry, and I gulped down my water. He shifted and smirked, "Are you hard, Joey?"

I choked and set the glass down.

He seemed delighted, and pressed, "Answer the question."

"Yes, sir." Was I ever.

"Good," he said and poured a tiny bit of wine in his empty glass, then offered it to me.

I didn't hesitate, letting the crisp, slightly sweet liquid slide down my throat. I set the glass down and smiled softly, feeling light.

"I have your word for you, Joey," he said suddenly.

I looked at him, unable to say anything.

"I would like to take you somewhere, show you some things. Things that might help explain everything a little better. Nothing will happen to you. You won't have to do anything," Gabriel said, his tone low. "Would you like to go?"

I didn't waste a second. "Yes, sir."

When the waitress returned, Gabriel informed her there would be no dessert, and handed her a credit card. He made quick work of signing the check, and though I couldn't see how much it was, I was willing to bet it had been quite expensive. I touched the wallet in my pants, unsure if I should at least offer to cover the tip. I probably didn't have enough.

I didn't say anything as we made our way back to the parking garage. I had noticed that Gabriel had a slight limp—maybe he had injured himself recently? Wait, he had said he had a bad knee.... I didn't ask for fear of prying. The valet retrieved the Camaro quickly, profusely thanking Gabriel for his generous tip.

"I need to make a quick stop first," Gabriel announced as we pulled out into the street.

We headed farther into the city, and Gabriel seemed to be looking for something or someone as we cruised down the streets. He apparently found what he was looking for and threw the car into park, then got out, the carton of food in his hands. I watched, entranced, as Gabriel walked to the alley and spoke to some homeless men huddled around some boxes. They shook hands and accepted the carton that Gabriel offered them.

What a wonderful gesture, I thought. It was nice to know there was a human being under that predator's disguise. I smiled to myself as Gabriel returned to the car. I was looking forward to whatever he wanted to show me, looking forward to so much more.

I couldn't wait.

Three

IT WASN'T a long drive to wherever we were going, but it was getting late, the night cool and clear. Time flies when you're having fun, I told myself, and I was truly enjoying the evening. As Gabriel pulled into a gated community, my head shot around in anticipation. The houses were spread apart, mostly on the shore of Lake Michigan. They seemed overly private, each surrounded by well-kept trees and bushes.

I was transfixed by the minimansion that Gabriel turned into, several spotlights accenting the stone walls. I could see the lake behind the house, the water dark and gray. As we pulled up, an elderly man dressed in livery arrived to take care of the Camaro.

Gabriel turned to me. "The important thing to remember is that there isn't anything in here that will harm you. Stay close to me. Everything will be fine."

"Yes, sir," I muttered, the nerves returning. Was this his house? He must have a lot of money to employ a private valet.

When we walked up to the door, Gabriel rang the bell. A few seconds later, it was opened, and an older man of about fifty appeared. My jaw audibly dropped to the floor—he was naked, with nothing but a black collar around his neck and some sort of plastic shield on his flaccid cock.

He tipped his head. "Nice to see you again, Master Gabriel. Please come in."

He turned and knelt on the floor, pressing his nose to the polished wood. I gasped—his behind was red with welts, as if he'd just received a harsh spanking, and he had some sort of plug in his ass. As he crawled across the floor, I pressed myself closer to Gabriel.

"It's okay, Joey," Gabriel reassured. "Come with me."

I swallowed grit and stuck close to Gabriel. I could hear my heart beating in my ears, the food I had eaten turning heavy. As we headed toward the stairs, I could see into the kitchen. There was a young man on his knees, some sort of biscuit on his nose, and the man above him was directing him to stay as if he were a dog. My knees were weak as I climbed the stairs. Although what I'd seen was shocking, it strangely felt... *normal*.

When we got to the second floor, a woman's voice caught my attention.

"Gabriel Mason," she cooed. "It's been a while."

Gabriel embraced her, kissing her on the cheek. "Mistress Victoria."

Gabriel shifted to the side, and I could see that the woman's attention had turned toward me. She was dressed in a slim black dress, her breasts nearly spilling out—knee-high boots conformed to her shapely legs. Her eyes were heavy with mascara, and when she looked at me, I couldn't help but shake in my shoes.

"This is your new boy, Gabriel? He isn't your type." She frowned, her lips plumping.

"Prospective boy." Gabriel grinned, giving me a once-over. "He's new to the lifestyle."

"Oh my. Keep him out of the basement, then." The woman arched a brow at Gabriel, her deep-scarlet lips pursing. "I thought training wasn't your thing."

Gabriel shrugged. "I'm looking for a quiet room so that we may talk."

She nodded. "Take the red room. I'll send in *It* for drinks."

And with that, she sashayed right past me, her eyes shrewd, as if she would enjoy crushing me under her boot. I swallowed hard, feeling vulnerable.

"Joey."

I turned my attention to Gabriel, my eyes wide.

"Come," he instructed, and I followed.

He led me into a room, the lights turned low. There was a big bed in the center dressed in red silk, and the windows were draped with red curtains. The furniture was all red and looked super plush. There was some sort of torture device in the corner, and I nearly tripped on the crimson rug as I eyed the thing warily.

"Ignore it," Gabriel said and took a seat on the couch. He patted the seat next to him. "Sit."

I obeyed, needing to get off my feet before I fell over. I'd been overloaded with everything. Fantasizing about all the whips and chains and bindings was one thing—seeing it up close in person? Terrifying.

"Look at me, Joey," Gabriel said, his voice stern. "Everything is fine. We're just going to talk a little more. I wanted you to see everything firsthand."

I dragged my eyes to Gabriel's. He was relaxing against the couch, his arms stretched along the backrest. He looked cool and collected, and the first two buttons on his shirt were unfastened as if he felt comfortable in these surroundings. I tried to calm myself, but I was shaking. I managed to ask, "What is this place?"

"Mistress Victoria's residence. To others who share the lifestyle, a place to relax and practice their desires without prejudice," he said, his tone even.

A knock at the door startled me, and Gabriel barked, "Yes?"

"Mistress said you require refreshments." A diminutive voice spoke.

"Come in," Gabriel said.

I watched, transfixed—it was the man who had opened the door for us. When he entered, he returned to the floor and proceeded to crawl toward us, his nose dragging along the ground. If this was an everyday thing for him, I was surprised he still had a nose.

"We will have tea with chamomile. If Timothy is in the house and is not occupied, send him this way," Gabriel ordered. "That is all."

"Right away, sir," the man said, then reversed direction.

I looked away, not wanting to be a leering jerk.

When we were alone again, Gabriel started speaking. "*It* is Mistress Victoria's house slave. She has a few. The slave who took my car also belongs to her."

House slave? My attention shot to the man next to me. Out of curiosity, I asked, "Do you have a... house slave?"

He chuckled, "No, I'm a one-slave kind of master."

That was good to know. I sometimes fantasized about doing several guys at once, but I knew that was one fantasy I didn't want to make reality. It was fun to think about, but I wanted just one man.

He was so close yet so far away, though I was sure I could feel the heat coming off his body. I parted my lips to ask about it, but I was unable to find my words. Whatever arousal had stayed with me all evening floated away, replaced by fear—was this the culmination of all my fantasies? Though I wanted to submit to a man like Gabriel, I didn't want to be viewed as... well, nothing, or be referred to as "It."

Gabriel must have sensed my apprehension, because he went on. "*It* is a nonconsensual slave—although that term is arguable. He consented to nonconsensual slavery. I know it's confusing. Joey, there are many degrees to this lifestyle. Some, such as Mistress Victoria, objectify their slaves, shape them into furniture, and for a few slaves, that works for them. Some people may dabble in submission, add a little spice to their plain lives. There is nothing wrong with this, but to those few like us, it is a daily thing, a lifelong choice. Hey, look at me."

I obeyed, Gabriel's gaze so intense that I had to struggle to keep it.

"What you need to ask yourself is, what are you? Do you just want to dabble in it every now and then, or are you looking for more—for the guidance of a master? Can you surrender yourself and all that you are to this person, trust them with everything, good and bad?"

I swallowed and suddenly felt cold. I let go of my breath. "I don't... know...."

Gabriel's eyes turned dark. "Get on the floor."

Though I was startled, I managed to slide onto the floor, not sure what Gabriel had in mind.

"A natural obedience," Gabriel remarked. "As a child, did you defy your aunt a lot?"

"No, sir. I was usually very quiet. We only had each other, and she had to work two jobs to support me, so I always made sure to help her as much as possible, even if it was just throwing the garbage out." I shook my head at my babbling. "I'm sorry, sir."

"And polite as well," he said, and pointed between his legs. "Come here."

I took a deep breath and crawled over to him. I didn't touch him, wasn't sure how to. He just sat there, looking down on me.

"Do you want to submit to me, Joey?" he asked, his voice a curl in the low light.

I opened my mouth to drag in some air and nodded.

"Are you going to touch me?" he asked, his tone even.

I felt my muscles tense to reach for him, but stopped, frowning.

"Why did you stop?"

"I, ah… how do you want me to touch you?" I wasn't sure if he wanted me to just touch his leg or maybe jack him off. This was all very confusing.

"What does it matter?" he said.

I frowned. "I would want to know what… feels best for you. I mean, if that's what you wanted."

"Do you want to please me, Joey?" he said.

"Yes, sir, very much," I said enthusiastically.

He leaned forward and gripped the back of my head, pulling me close to him. I could smell his dark cologne and something else, could see the stubble on his jaw. "I would fuck you right here, right now, on this couch. Would you let me?"

My cock awoke instantly, pressing against my pants. I croaked, "Yes, sir."

"Have you ever had anyone's cock inside you before, Joey?"

I gaped and managed to shake my head weakly.

"Yet, you would let me fuck you? I won't promise you I will be gentle. It might hurt. Will you still let me?" Gabriel growled, his grip on my neck tightening.

My mouth fell open, and I nodded.

"Why?" he asked.

"I want to make you feel good," I whispered. I was aware I'd become something else, something simple and primal, an animal, perhaps, caught up in the throes of arousal.

Gabriel seemed to like my answer and leaned back, releasing me. When he didn't say or do anything, I looked down. Yes, I wanted to submit to this powerful man, pleasure him, serve him, but….

"I don't want to be an *It*, sir," I said. "I want… a lot of what I've talked about, but I don't want to be nothing."

"Come sit up here, Joey," Gabriel said, and hit the seat next to him.

I didn't hesitate, returning to my spot, but then he was pulling me closer to him, his arms strong, solid, commanding. I accepted without protest. I was pulled against his chest, and he pushed my head against his shoulder.

"Do I scare you?" he asked, his voice deep.

I closed my eyes, liking him up against me. "Yes, sir."

"Good," he said, and I knew he was smiling. "Just relax. I know what it feels like to finally realize what you are. Though we are on opposite sides, we are a part of the same spectrum, molded from the same clay. I was twenty-three when I finally found out what I was, and when I did, I'd never before felt so complete."

I forced down a lump. "Would you tell me about it?"

A thumb brushed over my knuckle, and I sighed at the touch. I was terrified of Gabriel Mason, but at the same time, I thought I could trust him. I *needed* to trust him.

"Like you, I'd had thoughts of bizarre things starting from an early age. I imagined tying my high-school boyfriend up and whipping him until he was brought to tears. Those urges only intensified through college, but I kept my secrets to myself, feeling lost. I had always been private, hiding my desires, trying to conform myself to what society deemed acceptable. It made me miserable. Angry and frustrated, I started researching, looking for people who might share similar interests. I met up with a man named Dwayne Swanson. On the outside, he looked like your everyday, hardworking businessman, but underneath... he was me twenty years into the future. He showed me how to make my fantasy reality. He has owned his slave for over forty years now, and I am still shocked by how in love they are. They live the lifestyle 24-7 and have for years. It is amazing to me."

I listened to Gabriel's voice, my body relaxed, his chest solid, his body heat soothing. "I wasn't completely honest earlier, when I said I didn't have a word for my.... I know what it is, I think, but I've never had the courage to speak it out loud."

Of course, I'd done the research, browsed the porn sites. I inherently knew what I wanted my role to be, but recognizing it as anything more than fantasy was shattering. I had been raised as a good Catholic boy, taught to be respectful and helpful and—what I wanted wasn't something "good people" approved of. What I wanted would probably have given my pastor a heart attack.

"Can you say it now, Joey? After everything I've said and what you've seen?" Gabriel asked. When I didn't answer, he made me look at him, his authority evident in his eyes. "You have to be honest with yourself."

I parted my lips, tried to swallow—I had managed only a hoarse whisper. "Sex slave."

The corners of his lips twitched up, and I got the feeling he was proud of me for finally coming to terms with my role. "It's important to realize that sex doesn't define the role. There is so much more to it, though sex is a huge part of it."

A knock at the door startled me, and Gabriel snapped, "What?"

"Tea, sir. And you requested me?"

Gabriel set me aside, his expression becoming less serious. "Come in."

It wasn't *It* who walked in with a tray in his hands, but a man of about Gabriel's age, naked and with a collar around his neck, only it was white. He had dark hair and dark eyes but was light of complexion. He had a large tattoo slinking up his left hip—some sort of tribal design. He set the tray on the table in front of us, then tipped his head. I still hadn't gotten used to all the naked people roaming around.

"It's nice to see you again, Master Gabriel," the man said.

"Likewise, Timothy," Gabriel said, then fiddled with the teacups, handing me one. "How are you?"

I sipped at the tea, the liquid warming me instantly.

"Good, sir. And you?"

Gabriel shrugged. "Same as always. This is Joey. He is new to the lifestyle and is considering a contract."

Timothy looked at me, a teasing smile on his lips. "He looks barely old enough to drink."

I blushed and looked to Gabriel for guidance. He chuckled. "He isn't. I figured it would do him good to talk to someone of like mind."

Timothy nodded. "You want me to show him around a little?"

"Yes."

The man nodded toward the door. "Looks like you're mine, Joey."

I glanced, wide-eyed, at Gabriel, and he snickered. "It's fine. Nothing here will hurt you. Timothy will take good care of you."

I reluctantly set the cup on the table, then rose to my feet. Timothy closed the door behind me and smiled, his expression pleasant.

"Don't worry, I've got you. You have any questions, don't be afraid to ask. I know how overwhelming it is at first. You don't know which way is up or what the hell you are doing, but all you do know is how badly you want it. No—want isn't the right word. Need. You just need it," he said animatedly, fisting his hands.

Timothy's friendly demeanor calmed me, and I grinned. "Are you... Mistress Victoria's?"

He laughed and started walking. "No. I'm freelance, and I only do guys. Ah, she hired me to see that her guests are comfortable. I let them order me around a little, and if I choose, suck a cock or two, but I basically have all the control. If you haven't realized already, it's really the submissive that holds the power."

I nodded but muttered a "no" like an idiot.

Timothy seemed pleased, though.

"What about... ah, *It*?" I asked, really wanting to understand.

"Of course. I think the concept of nonconsensual slavery shocks most people new to the lifestyle. The important thing to remember is that *Its* slavery *was* consensual. His total slavery by Mistress Victoria is what gets him off—makes him feel... complete. Am I making any sense?"

I nodded enthusiastically. It did make sense, and now that Timothy had explained it, I felt a little better. He stopped at a door and told me to wait, then knocked. When he was granted permission, he peeked in.

"Master Darren. Daniel," Timothy said. "Master Gabriel has asked me to show a newcomer around a little, and I'm wondering if it would be okay if he witnessed your play for a moment? Great!"

Timothy nodded and led me into the room. My eyes immediately fell on the two men in the center of the room. There was a man tied to a large bedpost, his arms over his head, his teeth cutting into a red ball. His flushed cock was bound in rope, and he looked as if he were in pain.

The other man, dressed in nothing but leather chaps, grinned. "Welcome, new boy. Daniel would offer you greetings, except, well... as you can see, he is busy."

"T-thank you," I sputtered.

Master Darren turned to Timothy. "This is Gabriel's new prospective boy? He looks a little young."

Timothy chuckled and shrugged. Master Darren returned his attention to his slave and started whacking the man's cock with a crop. The man, whom I assumed was Daniel, arched and groaned against the ball.

Timothy leaned in to me and whispered, wagging his brows. "Daniel is a bit of a pain slut. It might look like he is suffering, but he is loving every minute of it."

I winced as Master Darren delivered a vicious slap to the man's tortured cock so that Daniel screamed against the ball. After a moment, he smiled, and when Master Daren asked if he wanted more, Daniel nodded his head furiously, begging in a slurred voice, drool cascading down his chin.

"See?" Timothy chuckled, then nodded toward the door. When we were back in the hall, he said, "There are a lot of degrees to the lifestyle. What gets one person off may be another's hard limit. It's all about finding what you like, and discovering it with a Dom is half the fun. Although Gabriel doesn't tend to take on *maybes*, he would be good to you. He is strict but fair and caring."

I frowned. "How do you know?"

Timothy licked his lips and grinned. "He took me on for a year. I had always been involved in the BDSM scene, but I wanted to experience a full 24-7 gig. He came highly recommended by Mistress Victoria, and I enjoyed every minute of it."

I smiled, suddenly realizing how lucky I was to have found Gabriel. Even if nothing happened between us, I knew I could go to him for advice, for direction. There was one thing I was frightened of, and that was getting involved with an abusive man. Even though I was new to this, I was pretty sure I would be able to tell the difference between a strict Dominant and a manipulative one. But what if I couldn't and put myself in a bad situation? Timothy's words soothed me.

Timothy showed me around a bit more, explained a few things, going into detail about consent and safety. When we entered the kitchen, there was a man sitting at the table sipping a bottle of water. I recognized the young man sitting next to his feet as the one who had balanced the biscuit on his nose. Timothy introduced us, and the man on the floor barked at me in greeting. Timothy explained to me that they were into "puppy play." I decided not to inquire further. On our way back up stairs, we passed a scene where Mistress Victoria was punishing *It*—he was receiving another harsh spanking. I winced.

By the time we got back to the red room, my mind was flooded with all I'd seen.

"Oh, and just between us… should Gabriel take you on, whatever you do, absolutely under no circumstance enter his house with shoes on. I swear, I can still feel his cane…. Anyway, good luck, okay? You're in good hands. I mean that."

"Thanks." I smiled. All through high school I'd had acquaintances—geeks and nerds, skaters, the typical "losers," but I'd never really felt as connected to them as I did to Timothy. It was nice to know there were people in the world that shared my kink.

When we entered, Gabriel was sitting on the couch with another man, chatting lightly. He beamed at me and motioned me over to the chair. "Everything go okay, Joey?"

"Yes, sir. It was… enlightening." I smiled.

"Good." He turned his attention to Timothy. "Thanks again. It was nice to see you."

Timothy tipped his head, but his attention was on Gabriel's friend. "Likewise, sir. If you want, you can pass my number on to Joey, should he have any questions."

"That's a good idea. I will."

When Timothy left the room, I settled in the chair and watched as Gabriel's guest got up. He looked to be a few years older, early wrinkles creasing his hazel eyes. "Well, I'll give you two your privacy. You'll let me know what happens with this one, hm? He is quite the handsome devil."

Gabriel laughed softly. "You know better than that. I'd say we are a pair of old gossiping ladies."

The man chuckled, then left, closing the door behind him, his eyes giving me a very thorough once-over.

"Joey?"

"Yes, sir?" I asked, giving him my full attention.

"Anything you'd like to ask?" he inquired, his eyes glowing in the low light of the room.

I wanted to ask so many things: What was puppy play, and did he like it? Did he enjoy torturing his slaves? What exactly did he like? I settled on "What if I want to explore these... feelings further?"

Gabriel licked his lips. "I had been thinking about that. What do you say to a trial of sorts? Spend a weekend with me—I'll introduce you to the role of a submissive, instruct you as I see fit, but I promise not to subject you to anything too serious. It would be good for you, I think, to experience it firsthand under controlled circumstances. Then you can decide for yourself if this is what you want. And if it is, you have the option of signing a contract with me. What do you say?"

I couldn't help the smile that creased my face. "It sounds great, sir. I want to do it."

Gabriel stroked his chin. "Wonderful... although there is something that I require. It is nonnegotiable. We will both be tested, and a full physical will be in order. A lot of the practices in this lifestyle are not 100 percent foolproof, and I want to make sure you are not subjected to additional risk. I know a good place, and the results should be delivered fairly quickly."

My shoulders slumped at having to wait, but I ultimately agreed. "Yes, sir."

"Good." Gabriel nodded, then checked his watch. "Boy... time flies. Well, I really hope you've enjoyed our evening."

"I did, sir. Thank you so much."

"You're very welcome." He grinned.

I touched the wallet in my jeans and bit my lip in indecision. "Sir, I—"

"Here is your first lesson," he started, his eyes alight. "A master always takes care of his slave."

I wanted to refuse. He had given me so much in only a few hours, but I decided to let it go. After all, I reminded myself of my words to Hanny when trying to convince her to let me pay some of the bills. If it made Gabriel feel good to provide for me, then that was all that mattered.

Gabriel had been insistent on driving me all the way home, and by the time we got back to my house, it was nearly eleven. The house was dark, with only the porch light's soft glow. Gabriel pulled against the curb and cut the engine.

"I'll send you all the info in the morning. It's a facility downtown, so you shouldn't have an issue busing it up there. My firm handles their financials, so I'll use a little magic to get the ball rolling. I suggest you take this time to think about everything you've seen."

"Yes, sir. Thank you." I smiled and took a deep breath, feeling comfortable with him for the first time.

"Good boy," he said, then got out of the car.

I followed, closing the door gently. Gabriel came around to join me and caged me in between his arms as he leaned into me. I couldn't help but press myself against the Camaro.

"I'm going to be honest. I'm really looking forward to this." He grinned, his eyes running up and down my body. Then he was touching my chin, making me look up at him. His lips came so close to me that I thought he might kiss me, but he whispered against my ear instead. "When you masturbate tonight, I want you to think of me. Think of me standing over you, a crop in my hand. When you come, you will call my name. Do you understand?"

"Yes... sir." I managed a hoarse response.

My cock had woken up, pressing against my jeans, needing to be touched. But just like that, he was gone, and before I realized what had happened, he was opening his door. "I'll call you in the morning with the details, so keep your phone close by."

"Yes, sir, good night," I managed.

"Good night, Joey." He smirked, then peeled away.

My legs were numb as I climbed the stairs to my bedroom, following the little trail of dim lights left on for me. I let my bag fall to the floor and collapsed on my bed. I quickly shed my clothes and smiled until my cheeks hurt.

My hand quickly found my hard cock, Gabriel's words stirring me. It was only a matter of seconds before I came, but it was massive.

Gabriel Mason—*Master* Gabriel. I did indeed call his name. Several times.

ℱour

FRIDAY MORNING, Gabriel had texted me saying that he couldn't call due to a business meeting, but he had provided me with the clinic's phone number and even was nice enough to look up some directions on the fastest way there. I got on my cell right away. They couldn't get me in that day but managed to squeeze me in on Monday. I could tell from the receptionist's tone that Gabriel had done a little strong-armed convincing.

I decided to make Monday my run-around day. I got up early, showered, and bused it downtown to the clinic. It was a nice place, and the staff scrambled to help me—courtesy of Gabriel's influence, no doubt. The doctor gave me a physical, and a nurse drew some blood. I was in and out in an hour. I was told, even with the rush on the lab work, it could take up to two weeks for me to get the results.

The waiting was going to suck, but I'd just have to deal with it.

I got to Simone University by noon and spent a while in their store. I found all the books I needed and even bought a university shirt in anticipation. My grand total was just over three hundred dollars. Luckily, the books didn't threaten to give me a herniated disk like my high-school cinder blocks had, so on the way back I stopped at Best Buy and drooled at all the MacBooks. I really wished I could afford one. I had done some budgeting and figured I could only spend about three hundred on a computer, which just wasn't enough. I wanted it to last a few years at least.

I dragged my feet out of the store. I knew eventually I was going to have to get another job. The only reason I'd left my part-time at the fast-food joint was because the hours conflicted with my classes and they'd been unwilling to negotiate. I'd had no other choice. Flipping burgers for the rest of my life was not on my to-do list, no matter how many times they named me employee of the month.

I made a last-minute decision to drop in at the local thrift store. I got lucky and found a nice Valentino long-sleeve for eight bucks, and some jeans. By the time I got home, it was getting dark. Aunt Hanny was on the couch, flipping through the channels.

"There you are. How was your day?" She smiled.

I licked my lips in thought. "My feet hurt."

She laughed. "Now you know how I feel, working at the diner."

I lost my playfulness. "When I'm a super famous novelist, I'm going to buy us a new house and that Beetle you've always wanted. And I'm going to get you an unlimited pass to some spa so you can enjoy a foot rub every day."

She giggled, sounding so young. "And what about that Shelby you've always wanted?"

"That too… but you first," I said, and dumped my load on the chair.

She got to her feet and pulled me into a big hug. "I'm so very proud of you."

I closed my eyes and inhaled her flowery perfume. She had no idea how her words made me feel. Of course, we both knew those dreams of shiny, expensive things would never come to fruition, but dreams were amazing things—they made you want to keep working for something, even if it seemed impossible.

"You hungry, baby?" she inquired, stepping away.

I shook my head. "Got something on the way home. I'm just going to go upstairs and relax. I've had a long day."

I accepted several smooches, then dragged myself to my room. I collapsed on my bed, exhausted. I peeled away the Band-Aid and cotton ball from my arm and discarded it in the wastebasket. Two weeks... soooo long, but worth the wait. I fished my phone out of my pocket and sent Gabriel a text to call me if he had the time.

I had just started to fall asleep when my cell chimed.

"Hello?" I croaked.

"Joey," Gabriel said. "Were you sleeping?"

"Sorry, sir... I had a busy day," I explained.

"I see. Did everything go okay at the clinic?" he inquired.

"Yes, sir. The receptionist said I should have the results in about two weeks," I explained, then kicked off my shoes, not realizing I was still wearing them.

"Good. My appointment is tomorrow," he said on a yawn.

"You sound tired too," I pointed out, then bonked myself in the head for stating the obvious.

He made a sound of acknowledgment. I heard something rustling in the background, someone talking... a door closing.

"Are you still at work, sir?" I inquired.

"Regretfully." He let out a big breath. "Distract me from my excruciating existence, Joey. Tell me about your day."

My lips quirked up of their own accord as I recounted my adventures in the city. I took a lot of time describing the campus to him, and from his questions, he seemed delighted. "I even bought a shirt."

"That's great, really," he said, and I could hear the smile through the phone. "Listen, it's been a long day for me, and I'm getting ready to head home. I'm going to let you go. Feel free to text me or call whenever you wish. I'd like to hear from you, okay?"

"Okay. Good night, sir," I said, wishing I could talk to him more.

"Good night. Oh, and Joey?"

"Yes, sir?"

He chuckled darkly. "Did you call my name?"

My cheeks burst into flames, but I grinned like a fool. "Yes, sir... three times."

"Mmmm... a lovely visual to fall asleep to. We'll talk soon. Good night, Joey."

I sighed heavily as he ended the call. I was looking forward to spending time with Gabriel Mason, wondering what he might do, what might happen.... I felt as if I would go crazy from the long wait, but like most things, I knew our time would come before I could blink. And like all good things, they were usually over all too soon.

Patience is a virtue, I reminded myself.

The clinic finally called on Friday morning to let me know my test results were in. The receptionist was kind enough to send the PDF documents to my e-mail address but let me know they usually didn't extend such favors. However, in this case, they were making an exception. I had to admit I was impressed with Gabriel's authority. I printed them out right away. I was clean—no surprise—and in good physical health. As soon as I had all the information, I called Gabriel.

"Joey," he said, his tone light. "You calling me this early in the morning can only mean one thing."

"Yes, sir.... I have my results. I'm good," I informed him, feeling my insides bounce.

"I received mine yesterday. How fortunate that you've got yours with the weekend upon us." He laughed.

I grinned and sighed.

"This weekend is good for you, am I correct?" he inquired.

"Absolutely, sir!"

"I will pick you up at nine o'clock tomorrow morning at the Midway station. Eat a light breakfast—toast or eggs. Bring with you your medical documents, a change of clothes—the necessities," he said.

"Yes, sir."

When we got off the phone, I collapsed in my bed and punched my pillow. I wasn't sure how I was going to sleep tonight with the excitement animating me, much less get through the day without putting holes in the walls from bouncing around. I had no idea what tomorrow would bring, but I knew it would be life changing.

MY HEART was pounding so hard, I thought it would break out of my chest.

We hadn't said much during the drive up to his house, Gabriel chatting lightly, asking how I was feeling. I had admitted to being a little nervous but was looking forward to serving him. He had smiled at that, leading me to believe he was as well.

As Gabriel led me up the stairs of his extravagant home, I couldn't believe this was finally happening. It was like a dream. Even though I'd talked about it with him and he'd introduced me to some of it back at Mistress Victoria's house, my mind couldn't wrap around the fact that my fantasies were about to become reality. Sure, it was just for two days, to see if the lifestyle was right for me... but oh my God.

It. Was. Happening.

Gabriel led me into the hall, where he bent down to untie his shoes. "Shoes are not allowed inside, ever. Do not let me find you stepping past the hallway with your shoes on—it is a severe infraction. Should you enter into my service, a pair of slippers will be provided for you, but you will rarely ever use them."

"Yes, sir," I said, and toed my All Stars off.

When we entered the front room, I understood why he was so strict about the no-shoes rule. The entire floor was covered in bright white carpet, and it looked recently installed—or just well kept. His house was ridiculously neat but posh, expensive furniture arranged around a huge television screen. There was even a fireplace with a deer's head over it, a large rack on display. The house was utterly beautiful, the kind of place modest families dreamed of.

"Did you kill that?" I asked breathlessly.

"Three years ago, yes. This way, Joey," Gabriel directed. "You will get a tour of the house later."

I followed, Gabriel leading me up the stairs and into an office, the smell of pine thick in the air. There were ceiling-high bookshelves with old, important-looking tomes, a small liquor bar, and a minifireplace. It was the type of office I'd want if I had loads of cash to blow.

He shrugged his jacket off and hung it on a hook. "I spend most of my time in here. As I said before, I often work on my off days. Sit down."

I took a seat on the leather couch, the cushions chuffing as it absorbed my weight. I was willing to bet the couch cost more than Aunt Hanny's beat-up Caddy. I watched as Gabriel went to sit at his dark, polished desk.

He asked, "You have something for me?"

"Yes, sir," I said and dug through my backpack, producing a manila folder.

Gabriel turned in his chair and fiddled with a safe, plucking out a similar manila folder. He came to join me on the couch, offering me the paperwork. I accepted and gave him mine. As I glanced at the papers, he looked through mine, then placed my folder into his safe. His report was nearly identical to mine—he was in good physical health and clean of any STDs. It was comforting to know he cared so much about something so important.

I frowned—apparently he was diabetic.

"Do I keep this?" I asked.

"Yes," he said, then moved over to his wet bar. He retrieved two squat glasses and filled them with some sort of amber liquid. When he returned to the couch, he offered me one, and I took it with shaky hands.

"Whiskey. It will relax you," he said and downed his in one go.

I followed his example, then coughed and couldn't help but make a face—man, it was strong. He chuckled and accepted the glass back.

"It is the sort of thing you develop a taste for," he explained, setting the glasses in the sink. "I prefer wine over strong alcohol, though. Maybe one day I'll take you wine tasting when you're legal."

I blushed at his wink. "I'd like that."

"We're going to talk a little, okay, Joey? I'm going to tell you what I want and expect from you. Then you will tell me what you think about everything and if you have any stipulations," he said but didn't give me a chance to respond. "As I've told you before, I don't normally go for such inexperienced men, so my instruction may seem a little harsh, but I demand total submission and loyalty. I will show you how to please me, and it will be your responsibility to learn quickly and execute my commands without hesitation and with devotion."

"Yes, sir," I confirmed, nervous excitement twisting in my gut.

He motioned to the folder in my hand. "Put it in your bag and get comfortable."

I obeyed, but relaxing was hard, even with the whiskey that warmed my insides.

"When you submit to me, you will be giving me use of more than just your body for my physical pleasure. Everything you do will be for my benefit, be it my laundry or lying on my floor with your legs spread just because I want to look at you. It's important that you understand you are here for my pleasure—what you want doesn't matter to me. If you're good, you'll be rewarded. If you're disobedient, you will be punished. I'm going to be honest, it won't be all fun and games. There will be many times when you might not like me. A lot of *maybes* come into this life thinking it's going to be fun. That's a big misconception. If you please me, you will be given pleasure as I see fit, but if you disappoint me, you will experience pain and humiliation."

As Gabriel spoke, everything spun around me in a jumble of confusion. My heartbeat was loud in my ears, and my lungs hurt— this was really happening....

"Any questions, Joey?" Gabriel inquired. When I opened my mouth and nothing came out, he went on, "Just to clarify what I touched on before. I want you to willingly submit to me because you want to. True power is given, not taken. Though you will belong to me, you are not an *It*. I take pride in my slaves, and I want them to be the best they can be, proud to serve their master."

That was exactly what I had wanted to hear. I sighed and closed my eyes. "Thank you, sir."

"Do you want to ask me anything?" he pushed. "Anything. This is the time when we set the conditions and rules. Is there anything that terrifies you? Your safety is my highest priority, and I need to know if there is something that might jeopardize that. Any allergies?"

I mulled over his words for a moment and shook my head. There might be one thing, but it was so silly, I felt embarrassed to mention it. "No, sir."

"I'm going to talk about safewords now. There may be a time or two in these next few days that I take you to a place you're not comfortable going to yet. Very early in the relationship, it's about getting to know one another—what I expect of you, what you can tolerate. If you feel like you're getting close to that place, you will say the word 'yellow,' and I will back off. I don't want you exploiting this word to back out of a punishment, but I also don't want you withholding it due to fear of disappointing me. Do you understand? You must be absolutely honest."

"Yes, sir, I do." I nodded, biting my lip.

"As for another word—'omega'—it is the end of all. If at any time you feel that this is not for you, you say this word and it all ends. I stop. We go our separate ways with no hard feelings. You must be very careful, though. If you even think about calling it out, then you need to seriously consider if this is what you want for your life. Do you understand the importance of what I am telling you?"

"Yes, sir."

"Good. Any questions? Concerns? Now is the time to speak."

I took a long minute to think but couldn't come up with anything. "No, sir."

"Should concerns arise in these next two days, you will voice them so that we may discuss them. Understood?" He drilled his eyes into me, entirely serious.

"Yes, sir."

Gabriel's lips quirked up. "Are you ready, Joey? Are you ready to submit to me?"

The words pierced me, stabbing me in the heart. My cheeks heated, and my stomach tumbled. This was it. "Yes, sir. I'm ready."

Gabriel didn't say anything and got up, disappearing from the room. I took a deep breath to try and steady myself, but my heart was pounding hard. I was aroused and fearful at the same time—such a strange combination. Gabriel's quick return startled me, and he closed his office door behind him. My eyes went right down to his hand—he was gripping a riding crop, the leather looking menacing in his strong hand.

Oh God.

"Stand in the middle of the room," he commanded, then took his seat on the couch.

I got up on shaky feet and took my place. I shuffled a bit, put my hands in front of my erection, unsure of the proper way to stand.

"When you address me it will be with respect. If I detect any sarcasm in your tone, you will receive an instant ten lashes with my cane. When I ask you a question, you will answer quickly and address me as sir. Understand?"

"Yes, sir." My voice was so hoarse.

"Remove your clothes and set them neatly on the chair," he said, motioning to a small chair next to a bookcase.

I hesitated for a moment. Of course, I knew getting naked in front of Gabriel was part of the deal, but I was self-conscious. I managed to peel my shirt over my head and push my pants down my legs. I folded them with great care, then set them on the chair. I resumed standing.

"Is there a problem, Joey? Did you not understand the order?" Gabriel asked, his tone angry.

I sputtered and looked at my boxers. "N-no, sir."

I took a deep breath and shucked them down my legs, then set them on the pile of clothes. The cool air hit my naked body, and I felt myself blush even more. This was the first time I had ever been completely naked in front of another man. Would Gabriel approve? I was scared that he might find something he didn't like.

He startled me by getting up and proceeded to circle around me like a hungry predator, his eyes all over my body, as if he were touching me with his hands. The small, blunt end of his crop touched me under my chin, and I looked up at him. His expression was loose but focused—he was completely in control.

"You will spend the majority of your time with me naked so that I may have the pleasure of looking at you whenever I choose. You are a good-looking boy, and I would not have you hidden from me. You have a nice face, pleasant to look at. Lovely colored eyes devoid of defiance. I long for a time when you might look at me with love and adoration befitting a slave," he said, then ran that crop down my neck to the dip in between my collar bones. When it grazed a nipple, I hissed. I didn't particularly like my nipples played with. "A little skinny, but that can be corrected."

I closed my eyes as he circled behind me. His hand on my ass made me gasp, that heavy palm caressing my skin, kneading the flesh. It felt so nice, the foreign warmth making me harder. I could just imagine those strong hands spreading me as he fucked me for the first time.

57

"Round, plump ass, perfect for spanking. Strong legs. Looks like that track team did you good." He laid a slap on my behind, and I jerked forward from the shock but managed to remain where I was as he inspected me. He came to stand in front of me again and craned his head to the side. That crop skimmed down my shaft, grazing the head of my cock, and I moaned softly. "Nice cock, good size. The fuzz has to go, though."

I had wanted to say something, but all thought fled as he stroked me with the cool leather. I had to ball my fists, it felt so good. He tapped the sensitive glans with the crop. I gasped, and Gabriel chuckled darkly, the little sting only heightening the pleasure.

"Next time you come to me, you will be clean-shaven. Pubic region, chest, ass, and underarms. I don't mind the legs," he said, skimming his crop up my belly. "You will regularly undergo inspections and will incur serious infraction should I find fault. Do you understand?"

My voice was shaky. "Yes, sir." Luckily, I didn't have that much body hair, but shaving my pubes was... scary. I supposed all men dreaded having sharp objects next to their dicks, but if that is what Gabriel wanted, then I'd do it.

"Good boy," he purred. "Now I'm going to show you how to *present* yourself to me. It is the position you will most often find yourself in. When I call you into a room, you will present yourself for further instruction. When you return from a chore, you will present. Basically, when in doubt... present. Now, get on your knees."

I obeyed and knelt down, waiting for further command.

"Spread your legs. Your knees should be far apart, your toes touching. Sit back on your legs so that your balls touch the ground," he said, using his crop to guide me into position. "Sit straight, spine erect, your hands on your thighs."

That crop skimmed up my throat and to my chin, and I craned my head back to look at Gabriel.

"When I speak to you, I want your eyes on my face so that I know I have your attention," he said, looking so very tall.

"Yes, sir," I said, concentrating on his electric eyes. They were intense, focused. I knew he was enjoying this.

"It's important that you pay close attention to my instructions. I will only tell you once, and it is your responsibility to carry them out as I demand. I'm going to give you a small task now, so listen carefully. You will go downstairs. Next to the hallway door is a small table. You will find a black leather-bound book and a pen. Bring these back to my office and place them on the table behind you. You have one minute."

"Yes, sir," I confirmed and got up.

I exited the office and ran down the stairs. I located the table and retrieved the book and pen, then took the steps two at a time back up to Gabriel's office. I was quiet as I entered, placing the book and pen on the table next to the wet bar. I hesitated for a moment, then remembered what to do, getting back on my knees.

Gabriel circled around me, and something bit into my ass unexpectedly. I hissed.

"Toes touching," he growled.

"Yes, sir." I swallowed, wanting to rub the place where the crop had stung me. I managed to stay where I was, straightening my spine so I didn't receive any more lashes. I watched as Gabriel took a seat on the couch in front of me. He leaned back and set the crop down next to him.

"Retrieve the book and pen," he said.

I obeyed, then returned, making sure I was perfectly positioned. I couldn't put my hands on my thighs while holding the book….

"Place the book and pen in front of you. Generally, when I request something of you, you will give me the item first, then present yourself," Gabriel said.

"Yes, sir." I set the stuff down on the Aubusson rug and returned my hands to my legs, awaiting his next command.

"Open the book to the first page and write your name on the line," he said. I did as I was told and neatly signed my name. "You will see just above your name the words 'This book is the property of Gabriel Mason.' Everything you are belongs to me, including your mistakes. On the next page, you will find two columns. On the left is where you will keep a tally of points; on the right is a description of the infraction. Enter five points for incorrectly presenting yourself. As I've said before, I will only tell you once to do something."

I swallowed and did as he commanded, hating that I had already messed up. When I was done, I looked up, unable to hide the shame. What if I screwed up too much and Gabriel decided I wasn't worth his effort?

"Every week, the points will be tallied up, and if the total is over one hundred, you will incur a punishment. Anything over one hundred rolls over into the next week. If it is two hundred, you will incur two punishments for that week. I usually carry them out right away but reserve the right to save them for a later day. Also, depending on my mood, I may choose to round up your totals at the week's end, should you be under one hundred points. If for whatever reason you earn one hundred points before the weekend, I may issue a punishment right away."

I swallowed hard and looked down at the black leather. I only had two days with this man, but how many points was I going to collect? How many times would I disappoint him?

"Joey, eyes here," Gabriel commanded. When I looked at him, he started talking again. "It's important to understand that in the beginning, you will earn a lot of points. This time is about learning what I expect from you, modifying your behavior to please me. Since you have zero experience, you may very well earn a punishment before you leave tomorrow night. I want you to know that when I administer a punishment, it's because I want you do to better. I want you to succeed at pleasing me. Do you understand what I am telling you, Joey? Do not get discouraged when you earn points. Accept them, learn from them."

My breath hitched, his words inspiring confidence in me. "Yes, sir. I want to please you, sir."

"Good boy. You're doing well so far. Do you have any questions or concerns?" he inquired.

I bit my lip, deep in thought. "I'm afraid to disappoint you, sir."

"There will be times when you do, but use those times to improve your performance," he said.

I nodded. "Thank you, sir."

"Why do I punish you, Joey?"

"So I can do better, sir."

"Good boy. Now I'm going to show you another position you will use often," he said and got up, flipping the crop in his hands. "It is called *display*. Sit, then lean back and distribute your weight on your arms."

I obeyed, leaning back, Gabriel's crop skimming my thigh.

"Your feet should be on the ground. Spread your legs wide so that your asshole is visible," he said, tapping the sensitive skin between my thigh and cock.

I bit my lip, doing as he commanded, feeling a little weird at being so exposed.

"Get yourself hard."

I shifted my weight onto my left hand and grabbed my cock. I was semiaroused, and it was only a few strokes until my cock was stiff and standing. A gentle touch of the crop to my knuckle let me know to stop, and I evened out my weight on both hands.

"When I tell you to display, I want to see you aroused. With your youth, you won't have a problem with this." He grinned, touching the head of my cock with his crop. I gasped, the touch making my balls tight.

"I may have you stay in this position for a long time. It will be your responsibility to keep yourself hard constantly. Should I find that you are slacking, points will be given."

"Yes, sir," I said. I didn't see that as a problem, but I didn't know how I could stand going hours without release. Maybe if I was good and did everything to his specifications, he'd let me come today.

"Now, for another important position. It is called *offer*. Get on your hands and knees. Your head and shoulders should be pressed upon the ground so that your ass is in the air."

I swallowed, assuming the position. I felt his crop tracing a light path across my butt.

"Legs spread, feet pointed out," he growled, that crop tapping the inside of my thigh. "You will offer yourself to me this way. With your hands, spread your cheeks in offer."

I tried to swallow but could not.

"Is there a problem?" Gabriel hissed when I didn't immediately obey.

"N-no, sir," I sputtered and parted my ass, feeling so vulnerable.

"There is not a part of you I won't see, Joey. No crevice, no nook or cranny or hole I won't see, touch, or exploit," he said, his tone low and mischievous. "Should it please me to have you offer at the front window so that I may see you when I come home, then that is what you will do."

His words startled me. Just to drive home the point, he laid his crop against my asshole none too gently. The sting was quick, and I jerked forward, muttering an "Ow." The burn lingered for a few seconds but eventually faded to a dull ache.

"Your asshole is mine," Gabriel growled. "I will take it wherever and whenever I wish, whether by my cock or a pretty pink dildo. Do you understand?"

"Yes, sir," I responded, the first touch of fear coursing through me.

"What belongs to me?" he prompted.

"My asshole, sir," I said shakily.

"Say it."

"My asshole belongs to you, sir," I said as clearly as I could manage. I wouldn't deny that admitting that out loud was a turn-on, even if I harbored fear at being at Gabriel's mercy. At Mistress Victoria's house, he'd told me bluntly when he fucked me for the first time it might hurt, but I was hoping he'd be a little considerate. I thought he might have said it to scare me, but I wasn't so sure now.

"Good boy," he said, his voice softening. "I'm really enjoying this, Joey."

"I'm glad you are, sir," I said respectfully. After all, the only reason I was here was to please him.

I couldn't see what Gabriel was doing, but I heard the squeak of his office chair, so he must have sat down. He didn't say anything for several long moments, and I thought he was just watching me, enjoying the view.

"Go downstairs and into the kitchen. In the refrigerator, on the very bottom shelf, you will find several bottles of water. Retrieve one and bring it to me," Gabriel ordered.

"Yes, sir," I said and scrambled to my feet.

I made sure to close the door behind me and rushed down the stairs, sliding on the hardwood floor of the kitchen. I quickly located the fridge and plucked a bottle of Ice Mountain. I climbed the stairs and stopped in front of the office door. I took a deep breath and slowly let it out. When I was ready, I entered. Gabriel was sitting back in his chair, his fingers folded on his desk, watching me. I set the bottle on his desk, then presented myself.

I swallowed hard as he got up and inspected my position. When I didn't feel the bite of the crop, I assumed he was happy with my effort. I stared straight ahead, the clink of glasses sounding loud to my ears. Gabriel returned to his desk and cracked the lid of the bottle. He split the water between the two glasses, then handed me one.

"Thank you, sir," I said, took the glass, and sipped the cool water.

He leaned against his desk and took a drink, his lips moist. I wondered what they might taste like and if he'd ever kiss me. "Next time, before entering, knock and announce yourself."

"Yes, sir," I confirmed, then drank the water, moistening my throat. It was much needed, and I hadn't realized how thirsty I was.

I finished off the water, and he took the glass from me, returning it to the sink. "Better?"

"Yes, thank you, sir."

He returned to his desk, resting his behind against the heavy wood. He seemed to be mulling over something, his eyes narrowed on me. He tilted his head and ran his eyes up and down my body, that little quirk at the corner of his lips letting me know he was thinking of something wicked.

"Have you sucked a lot of cock, Joey?" he asked.

My dick jerked at the words. "Ah, a few, sir."

"How many is a few?" he inquired.

I shrugged. "Three."

"Did you like it? Be honest," he pushed.

"Yes, sir," I confirmed.

Gabriel gripped the tent in his pants, stroking his length with his thumb. "You've done very well so far. I think you are due a reward."

I heard myself moan but didn't say anything. My eyes fell to what he was doing, his erection pressing against the thin fabric of his slacks. I wanted to see it, touch it, taste it. I hoped he would let me.

"Come closer," he commanded. "But keep your posture."

I obeyed, walking on my knees. I touched his pants.

"No," he said firmly. "You will not touch me unless I have given you permission. I will not tell you again."

I quickly reined in my errant hand. "I'm sorry, sir."

I watched as Gabriel undid his zipper and pulled out his cock. It was bigger than I had imagined, red and flushed and heavily veined. Beautiful, really, and I knew it would own me whether it was in my mouth or in my ass. I wanted to experience both.

He reached for me and dug his fingers into my hair, pulling me closer to him. I instinctively opened my mouth to accept him, but he stopped me from taking his cock into my mouth.

"Stick your tongue out," Gabriel ordered.

I didn't hesitate, opening my mouth and extending my tongue.

"You will associate this posture with *accept*," he said.

I couldn't answer, not unless I wanted to close my mouth, and I deduced from the look in his eyes that he was allowing me to work it out for myself. I just hoped I had made the right decision. I simply looked at him, awaiting whatever he was willing to give.

"Good boy," he whispered, then pressed the tip of his cock against my tongue.

Still, I didn't move, didn't attempt to lick, even as much as I wanted to. It wasn't nearly enough, but I accepted what he had given me. He rubbed the underside of his glans along my tongue, and I could smell his manly scent. It was a mix of dark cologne and his natural musk.

"You want to taste your master's cock?" he asked.

I made an indecipherable sound, and he smirked, giving me a little more. It still wasn't enough, and I actually whimpered.

A wicked light entered his eyes. "Beg me for it."

"Please, sir... let me suck your cock."

"Why?" he asked.

My instinctual response was to tell him I really wanted to, but I realized he was testing me. What I wanted didn't matter. "To please you, sir. Make you feel good."

"That's right. Now, suck me good and don't let me feel your teeth," he ordered.

As I closed my lips around Gabriel's cock, I groaned in triumph, my own dick thickening. I was so monstrously aroused that there was a dull ache in my balls. I needed to come so bad. He controlled me with his hand in my hair, not letting me gain much leeway, but at least I got to feel his veiny length in my mouth. His skin was slightly salty, the precum a little bitter.

"Show me how bad you want to please your master," he said, and released me.

I didn't hesitate, swallowing Gabriel's cock, bobbing my head back and forth as I tried to pleasure him. Apparently I was doing something right, because he gasped, then groaned as I worked his cock. I tried to take more of him, wanting it all, and—

A sudden sting fired off in my hand, and I pulled my arm away from him.

"I told you, no touching without permission," Gabriel hissed.

I retreated to apologize, not realizing I had grabbed onto his leg, but his hand fisted in my hair, keeping his cock in my mouth. "Hands behind your back, grip your wrist."

I mumbled a "Yes, sir" and did as told. He held my head still and began pumping my mouth, going deeper than I had dared to take him. When I gagged, he chuckled but didn't stop thrusting in long, slow motions. I choked, and he pulled out, giving me a much-needed break.

"Take a deep breath," he said.

I did as instructed and parted my lips as his cock was slipped back into my mouth. I concentrated on trying to control my gag reflex, but he didn't gain much access. I wished I could take more. I knew he wanted to bury his cock to the hilt, but tears had started to pool in the corners of my eyes, and my breath was uneven.

"There will come a time when you will be able to take me down your throat, your lips pressed to my skin," he said hoarsely. "Don't get discouraged. Like all things, skills are learned through practice."

His words soothed me, filled me with hope and fantasies of him instructing me on how to take him down my throat. I couldn't wait. I really wanted to learn how to please him this way. When I gagged again, he took his cock from my lips, and I wanted to beg that he let me try again.

"Accept," he said.

I immediately stuck out my tongue, and he tapped his heavy dick against it. He started stroking himself, his glans resting on my tongue. I watched as his hand moved, watched in awe as his face tightened, his breath hitching. He craned his head back, the muscles in his neck tightening, and when he groaned, my cock jerked at the sound. He was a feral animal, a beautiful beast. He came in my mouth, one hot spurt after another. It wasn't entirely pleasant, but it was Gabriel, and I had no complaints.

When he was done, I swallowed and watched, entranced, as his body loosened. He looked down on me, his face relaxed. "Did I tell you to swallow?"

My cheeks heated. "I, ah… no, sir."

"Clean my cock, slave," he ordered.

I obeyed, sucking on the head, cleaning the salty bitterness from his dick, washing it away with my saliva. He ran the glans along my lips, my eyes on him, and I could see that he was pleased with my efforts even if I had swallowed out of turn. That look meant a lot to me. I was glad I had pleasured him.

He pulled away and stuffed his cock back into his pants. "Retrieve your book and pen."

"Yes, sir," I confirmed and grabbed the items.

When I presented myself with the book and pen on the floor in front of me, he spoke. "Enter ten points for touching me without permission, then five points for swallowing when I did not tell you to do so."

"Yes, sir." As I wrote in the book, I felt disappointment fill me. Three infractions so far, twenty points—three times I had failed him.

"Joey." When I dragged my eyes to him, he said, "Learn from your mistakes. Every week, when points are tallied and before punishment is given out, we will sit down and discuss your infractions so that you will understand how you can perform better."

"Yes, sir. Thank you, sir," I said, trying to keep myself composed.

He came forward and touched my head, pressing my face against his leg. I moaned as he petted me, the warmth of his body coming through his clothes. I wanted to reach out and touch him so badly but managed to keep my palms on my thighs.

"You are doing very well, Joey," he complimented.

"Thank you, sir," I whispered and concentrated on the moment. His fingers running through my hair felt so very nice—I never wanted it to stop. But like everything, all good things came to an end.

He stepped away, and I nearly fell forward, craving his touch, but managed to right myself.

"Take your book and pen and follow me downstairs," Gabriel ordered, retrieving his crop.

"Yes, sir." I followed him out of the office and back down to the first floor, my eyes on his body.

He stopped in the living room and turned to regard me. "Your book will be left in either of two locations. The desk in my office or the table next to the hallway. Should I find it in any other place, you will be given five lashes with my cane for carelessness. Your point book is very important. If you don't respect it, then you don't respect me. Place the items there now, then present yourself on the side of the couch."

"Yes, sir," I confirmed, and set the book and pen on the table, then hurried over to the couch.

"Walk, don't run," he commanded. "Your eagerness to serve me will be in your eyes, not in your feet."

"Yes, sir." I forced myself to slow down, then presented myself next to the couch, the carpet scratchy against my balls.

I waited for further instruction as Gabriel took his seat on the couch directly in front of me and turned the television on. I didn't look away and kept my attention on him, but some sort of newscast caught my ears. I didn't pay much attention to it, my concentration on the man on the couch. He was relaxed, his arms stretched along the back, his eyes on the mounted screen.

I watched as his face went through different expressions, from anger to frustration to disbelief. He called the newscaster a bloody idiot several times, and he looked as if he wanted to strangle the man. I had gotten the gist of his ire—it was about the sequestration. Apparently, Gabriel didn't like the newscaster's opinions on the matter.

"Do you take an interest in politics, Joey?" he asked without looking at me.

"Ah, some, sir."

"What is your opinion on the sequestration?" he inquired.

I bit my lip, wondering how to word my thoughts without angering him. "I'm mostly worried about the cuts to programs that help the disabled and impoverished more than anything. No offense, sir, but, ah… sometimes I think the rich guys are a bunch of crybabies."

His attention turned toward me, and I thought I might have pissed him off. Instead, he smirked. "I couldn't agree more."

I sighed, relieved. He didn't say anything else, and I relaxed a little, knowing I'd pleased him in some small way.

Five

I WASN'T sure how much time had passed, but as I sat here, I couldn't help but start rocking slightly. Gabriel was caught up in his program, and I didn't want to disturb him. I closed my eyes, concentrating on holding my bladder—that water had seemed to go right through me.

"Is there a problem, Joey?" he inquired, his tone devoid of emotion.

"Ah, I'm sorry, sir, but I... really need to pee," I said softly.

"Unlike some masters, I do not hold bathroom and food rights hostage. Should you need to relieve yourself, simply ask, but it will be your responsibility to manage your time. I would not be very happy should you need to use the bathroom when you are in the middle of pleasuring me," he said. "There will be time when I require nothing of you that you may take the opportunity to attend yourself."

"Yes, sir," I confirmed, then hesitated. "May I use the bathroom, sir?"

"You may. It's down the hall on your left."

I quickly found the bathroom. Actually, it was more like a minispa with a large shower and roomy space complete with marble sink and a black commode. It was probably the size of my bedroom, and my mattress would comfortably rest in the bathtub. I smiled with contentment as I relieved myself. I didn't want to spend too much time in the bathroom, so I quickly but thoroughly washed my hands. Gabriel might need my services soon, and I wanted to be available. I checked myself in the mirror. My hair was tousled, the locks going every which way from Gabriel's fingers. I didn't bother taming it.

When I returned to the front room, Gabriel was still watching the news program, muttering curses. I took the proper position and waited.

"Are you hungry, Joey?" Gabriel asked, his attention still on the television.

I touched my belly. "No, sir."

"Are you sure? It's almost two, and you've had a light breakfast."

"Yes, sir," I confirmed. I should probably eat something, but my stomach was a little upset from nerves. I didn't want to make it worse.

"Well, I am," he said, then turned his attention toward me. "Pay close attention—I'm in the mood for a ham sandwich. On the left side of the counter is a bread box, and inside you will find a loaf of wheat bread. Three slices of ham, one slice of cheese, two slices of tomato, which are in the bottom left drawer, and heavy lettuce. The tomato should be sliced perfectly—not too thick, but not thin. No mustard or mayonnaise. On the very first shelf to the right, you will find a pitcher of iced tea. Do not add anything to it—this is very important. The cups and plates are in the cabinet above the bread box. Cut a lemon into eight slices. The sandwich and lemons should be on separate plates, and don't forget a napkin. In the cabinet under the bread box you will find a tray. Place everything on there and bring it to me. Whatever dishes you dirty will be placed into the left side of the sink."

"Yes, sir," I said and got up, reciting everything in my head. I knew the attention to detail was a test, and I was determined to pass.

I got the tray first, then located two plates, one for the sandwich and a smaller one for the lemons. I retrieved two slices of bread, making sure to redo the twisty tie, and then collected everything from the fridge: three slices of ham, one slice of cheese. Two slices of tomato and lots of lettuce later, I was sure I had made it precisely to Gabriel's instructions. I poured the iced tea and cut the lemon. I took a moment to make sure the counter was clean and all dirty dishes were in the sink. I took a deep breath, then carried the tray into the front room.

Gabriel pointed at the push table to his side. "Set it here."

I did as instructed, then returned to my spot. I watched intently as he pulled the push table to him, then inspected my work. He took a bite of the sandwich, then gave me a thumbs-up. I beamed.

When he turned to his iced tea, he frowned. "Come here, Joey."

I swallowed hard and obeyed.

"Where did you learn how to slice lemons? This wedge is too thick, makes it hard to squeeze, while the other is too thin, causing it to mash when I squeeze. I expect you to do better next time."

"Yes, sir," I said bashfully.

I felt embarrassed that I had botched so simple a thing, but Gabriel was giving me another chance to do it correctly. I returned to my position and watched him eat, his jaw working as he chewed his food. He ate with elegance, each bite careful, each sip of the tea savored. I got the sense that he had grown up in a rich household where manners were important and ingrained from a very young age. It was also in how he spoke, his words carefully pronounced. I wanted to ask but was afraid to speak out of turn.

Eventually, he wiped his lips and hands, balling the napkin on the plate. He muttered a curse, then turned the television off. When he stood up and stretched, he said. "Retrieve the tray and bring it into the kitchen."

"Yes, sir," I said and collected the tray, following him into the kitchen.

I unloaded the dirty dishes into the sink.

"Put the tray back where you found it," he said, then started going through the fridge.

"Yes, sir."

I slid the tray back into the cabinet carefully. When I was done, I wasn't sure if I should present or not.

"Joey," Gabriel said, his face tight. "Come here."

I reluctantly dragged my feet to where he was standing with the fridge open. He pointed at the lunch meat drawer.

"One of these things is not like the other," he said.

I bit my lip and leaned in to see what I had messed up. I gasped and blushed. I retrieved the open package of ham and sealed it, then put it back in the drawer. I looked at Gabriel sheepishly. "Sorry, sir."

"This is how things spoil," he said adamantly. "It's pointless waste."

I nodded. "Aunt Hanny says the same thing."

He cocked a brow. "A bad habit, I see. You've disrespected my property. What do you think should be done?"

I did a fish impression, my cheeks burning. I wasn't sure what he was asking, what he wanted from me. I swallowed hard, trying to think of the right words to say. "Points, sir?"

"Go get your book," he commanded, then closed the fridge.

"Yes, sir," I responded weakly. I retrieved my book and pen, then returned to the kitchen. I had nearly forgotten to present myself and scrambled to the floor. The last thing I needed was more points.

"How many points do you think you deserve?" he inquired, leaning against the counter.

I looked at the black leather. I wasn't sure why he was asking me. Wasn't it *his* right to administer points and punishment?

"Joey."

I snapped my attention back to him. "Yes, sir?"

"Do you understand why I am asking you?"

"No, sir," I responded, feeling lost.

"Did you not disrespect my property and, in turn, me? Do you agree that there should be a penalty?" he asked, his tone even, patient.

"Yes, sir," I said. He didn't say anything further, but I could see from his patient expression that he wanted me to work this out. "I feel... bad for disappointing you, sir. I should be... penalized."

"When Timothy was under my command, he had once come to me admitting a mistake that I hadn't noticed. Why do you think that was?"

I thought about it. Now that Gabriel had put it like that, this lesson made sense. "Because he respected you, sir. Because... it was his duty to please you in all ways, and if you had noticed, punishment would have followed. You didn't... but he wanted to be a good slave... and informed you so it could be... corrected?"

"Very good, Joey. Hiding your mistakes means you don't respect me or my command." Gabriel appraised, his lips lifting just a little. "Do you wish to do better, Joey? How many points do you think you've earned?"

I swallowed a lump in indecision. What would appease Gabriel? "Twenty... sir?"

The man arched a playful brow. "So many? Are you sure?"

"I want to do better, sir!" I cleared my throat and looked down. "Sorry, sir."

"Then add it into the book," Gabriel said.

"Yes, sir." I did as told, hating that I had already amassed almost half a week's worth of allowed points. Looked like I would be due a punishment before I left tomorrow night.

Gabriel left the kitchen momentarily, and I sighed. I had to admit to myself that the points were well deserved. Gabriel returned, his crop in his palm, and I looked to him for explanation.

"Return your book to its proper place, then bend over the counter," he said, remarkably at ease.

My breath hitched, and I whispered a "Yes, sir." I quickly returned the book and pen to the table, then slunk back into the kitchen. I bent over the counter, the marble cool against my naked skin. I flinched when his hand touched my ass, his fingers kneading the flesh softly.

"I am happy that you understand the lesson. More importantly, you were honest in your desire to please me. You could have said five points, perhaps ten. Why do you think you deserve twenty?" he said, his tone suddenly comforting.

"Ah... I did not mean to disrespect you, sir. Even if it was unintentional, I... I should be penalized for doing so," I whispered, that warm palm calming me. "I am here to serve you, and I really, really want to make you happy, sir."

"Do you want to make amends right now?" He arched a brow as if this was going exactly the way he planned.

"Yes, sir," I said, closing my eyes against his touch. I hissed when the little tongue of his crop skimmed up my crack, the touch featherlight. "Please, sir...."

"Spread your legs and stick your ass out," he ordered.

I did as I was told. The first spank was startling, and I jerked. The sting was hot, and I couldn't help but whimper. Another came, this time on the other side of my ass. "Ow."

"Does that hurt? Do you want me to stop?" he inquired, rubbing the sting away with the tip of his crop.

"It hurt, sir," I said. Something deep twisted inside me, I wasn't sure what it was, and before I could stop myself, I said, "You should give me more, sir."

"More, Joey? Why?"

I didn't hesitate. "Because I disrespected you, sir. I should be punished."

The third swat wasn't as startling, but it did sting, and I winced against the pain.

"Good boy," he said softly, his palm running up my back to push my body against the countertop. I relaxed, the cold marble pressing against my cheek. Instinctively, I pushed my ass out farther. "There is one thing you should know should you decide to submit to me on a regular basis. In the beginning, you will have a very sore ass. From now on, every spank I administer with anything other than my hand, you will count out. Understand?"

"Yes, sir," I confirmed.

"Let's practice," he said, and I could hear the tease in his voice.

I groaned against the lash and managed to grind out, "One, sir."

He didn't give me a chance to recover, and I barked out the count. He chuckled, enjoying the whole thing, and though it hurt a little, I wanted more if it would please him. Honestly, it wasn't that bad, nothing compared to what I thought he might be capable of.

He gave me three more, and I moaned against the counter.

"Good boy," he said, rubbing my ass with his palm. "Your determination in accepting your punishment has made be happy."

"Thank you, sir," I mumbled, unable to keep the smile from my lips.

A shrill ring interrupted us, and I craned my head around to see Gabriel pull his cell phone out of his pocket. He looked at the screen, his expression turning hard.

"Mason," he hissed.

I stayed where I was, my ass out in the air, as he growled and cursed at whoever was on the phone. As I listened to him berate the person, I relaxed against the counter, the cool marble against my skin contrasting with the heat on my ass. It was strange, but I wished he would give me a little more. After the initial sting, the lingering sensation felt kind of nice.

Gabriel snapped his fingers at me to get my attention, then curled his finger toward him. I followed without hesitation as he hoofed up the stairs, still yelling at whoever was on the phone. He barged through his office door, and I closed it behind me, then presented myself as he took his seat at his desk. He was angry about something, his eyes bright with fury, his face tight. As his harsh words bounced around the walls, I shivered, afraid of him for the first time. I hoped that I never made him so angry.

He dug through his desk, finding a paper. "The fucking notice was sent out two weeks ago, Riley. What the fuck was your department doing? No—don't answer that, just fucking fix it."

He snapped his phone shut, then threw it across the desk. His piercing gaze fell on me, and he snapped, "Come here. Bend over on my desk."

I stumbled to my feet, not wanting to make him wait a second. I pressed my body down to the cool wood, displaying my ass for his pleasure. I felt him come closer, his knees touching my legs. Then his hands were on my ass, the caress arousing me. He used his feet to tap my ankles, and I spread my legs.

"I did not mean to snap at you. Did I scare you?" he inquired, his tone calm.

"Ah… you seemed upset, sir."

"That's not what I asked. In any event, I did not mean to do so, and I apologize. My firm is insistent on hiring incompetent assholes who try to blame their mistakes on others. I detest such people," he growled.

"I'm sorry, sir. Is there anything I can do to… make you feel better?" I asked softly.

He chuckled, laying a spank to my left cheek with his heavy palm. "Yes, there is. Let us finish what we started," he said, his voice evening out.

"Yes, sir," I said.

When the familiar flat tip of the crop touched my skin, I moaned. It skimmed across my ass cheeks, then followed my crack down to my ball sac until I gasped. Gabriel was clearly pleased, that dark laugh penetrating me.

"Do you remember where we left off, Joey?" he inquired.

"Five, sir."

"You want more, Joey?" he pushed, his voice low and dangerous. "Or do you think five is enough?"

"Yes, sir," I confirmed. "I would like more, sir."

He growled softly, apparently liking my answer. The crop bit into my ass cheek, and I hissed, but it was quickly rubbed away by Gabriel's palm.

"Six, sir."

"Did you like that?" he purred.

I moaned.... I was surprised to find that I did. "Yes, sir."

"Thank me," he said.

"Thank you, sir," I responded, preparing for another.

"Why did you thank me, Joey?" he inquired.

I opened my mouth to speak, but nothing came out. I had wanted to say because he had told me to, but his tone hinted at something else.

"I will have you know that even though I own you, your body, your actions, I want you to be able to think for yourself. I want you to be able to make decisions—will you do something half-assed and risk punishment or complete the task to your best ability to please me? Regardless of what you might think, you do have choices. You don't have to like this just because you think it will please me more. You are allowed to hate it, but that doesn't change the fact that it will be done. All you have to do is accept," he said, his tone comforting. "Now tell me, do you like it, Joey? Do you like the way the little sting arouses you. Are you hard?"

I could hardly breathe—it was amazing the way he burrowed deep into me, got into my thoughts and desires with only a few words. I moaned softly. "Yes, sir, I'm hard. I... really do like it."

He chuckled. "Good. So, why are you thanking me?"

"For allowing me a little... pleasure and for... letting me please you," I said.

"Good boy," he praised.

I smiled, only to suck my breath in as he laid another spank on my opposite cheek. On instinct, I said, "Seven... and thank you, sir."

His hands massaged my ass, the sting creating a nice sensation.

"Display yourself on my desk," he ordered.

"Yes, sir," I confirmed and peeled myself off the wood. The desk was cool against my spanked ass as I got up on it, evening my weight out on my hands and feet. I spread my legs. I didn't need to stroke myself. I was already hard, my cock standing straight out as if begging for Gabriel's touch.

Gabriel was sitting back in his chair, his eyes hooded, his lips quirked with a wicked smile. He scooted in and gripped my thighs, pushing my legs farther apart until I felt my muscles stretch. His fingers were warm against my thighs as he explored me. When he cupped my nut sac, I arched my spine and gasped. I'd only had one other guy touch me like that, but Gabriel's touch was explosive.

I swallowed hard as he flicked the crop lightly against my balls.

"That scare you?" he asked.

"A little, sir," I admitted. It was one thing to have my ass spanked, but my balls?

The crop slapped my thighs, not too hard, but it was shocking to feel the sting there. Slowly, Gabriel worked his way toward my ball sac. I watched, entranced, as that tool worked in rapid repetition, getting closer. I bit my lip in indecision. I wanted to pull away but was curious at the same time.

Just like that, Gabriel pushed himself away from me and relaxed against his chair.

"Stroke yourself," he ordered.

"Yes, sir," I confirmed and gripped my cock. I didn't get more than a few strokes off before Gabriel slapped his crop against my knuckle.

"Slowly," he said. "I've told you to stroke yourself for my viewing pleasure, not because I'm allowing you to come. Everything you do is for my benefit, Joey."

"Yes, sir." I forced myself to go slowly, from base to tip, my glans popping in and out of my fist. It felt ridiculously good, the pleasure heightened by being watched by Gabriel. He licked his lips, and my confidence soared. I had to remind myself that I was doing this for him.

"That's it, Joey. Entice me," he said hoarsely. "You're a handsome, boy. Don't be afraid to exploit it. You want to please your master, don't you?"

I managed to mumble a "Yes, sir" and pushed my hips up, unable to help the moan that was ripped from my lips. As a bead of precum oozed from my cock, I squeezed, the moisture sliding down my hand. Gabriel's crop touched my thigh gently, sliding across to my nut sac. I gasped as tension built in my balls. I was determined to beat it back, to keep on with the show, but I was ridiculously aroused.

"You getting ready to come?" Gabriel asked.

"Yes, sir," I gasped.

He tapped my hand with the crop. "Stop."

I obeyed instantly, peeling my hand away. I watched, amazed, as my cock flinched, needing stimulation. When the orgasm eased a little, I took a deep breath.

"I'm going to have to train you on how to hold your orgasms. It's only been… what, a minute?" he said, his eyes alight.

I blushed. "Sorry, sir."

"Don't apologize for something you have no control over. I was the same way when I was your age," he said, then touched my glans with the tongue of the crop.

I groaned, and he chuckled.

"Start again," Gabriel ordered.

"Yes, sir." I gripped my cock and resumed masturbating, trying to hit the head as little as possible, but the orgasm quickly rebuilt. I concentrated on holding it back, tried to think of disgusting things like creepy-crawly things.

"If you feel you're too close, stop yourself," he said. "I have not given you permission to come, and to do so without my consent is a severe infraction."

"Yes, sir," I gasped, and pulled my hand away. I couldn't help but thrust up into the air and moaned in desperation.

"Good boy," he praised, running the crop along my thigh.

I closed my eyes as the tool roamed across my skin, grazing my taint, to settle against my asshole. He tapped lightly, hardly more than a spank, but I gasped.

"You've told me no one has fucked you, but have you ever played with your ass, Joey?" he inquired.

"Sometimes, sir." I managed to speak, that light tapping keeping the orgasm close to the surface.

"Fingers? Dildos? Be more specific," he commanded.

"Fingers, sir," I whispered, grinding my teeth.

"Did you like it?"

"Yes... sir," I said shakily. "Felt weird at first."

Gabriel made a sound of acknowledgment, his eyes going dark as something wicked flashed across his face. He leaned down and riffled through his desk drawer, producing some sort of black... dildo? It looked like a bunch of balls piled on top of one other. It wasn't very large—its widest point about the width of two fingers—but it was intimidating.

"While awaiting your test results, I bought this in anticipation. It's been sitting in my drawer for almost two weeks. Every time I open it, I see this and think about what it might look like sliding in and out of you."

My jaw seemed to dislodge from my skull, the words so very wicked and erotic I could hardly breathe. Those electric eyes that were on the dildo flicked to me. "I'm assuming you took a shower this morning."

"Yes, sir," I managed, my eyes widening as the dong came closer. When the smallest ball touched my thigh, I jerked. The rubber was cool, smooth, and Gabriel languorously dragged it to my taint. I hissed as it slid down to graze my asshole. I had to bite my tongue as the rubber teased my entrance, my cock still hard and aching.

Gabriel took it away, only to squirt some lube on the tip. I watched with wide eyes as it was brought back between my legs. I took a deep breath, the cool slickness startling. He didn't push it into me, just spread the lube all over my crack, teasing my entrance with the ball until I couldn't help but press against it.

"You want it, Joey?" he rumbled.

"Yes, sir... please," I whimpered.

He pressed lightly against my asshole, and the first ball slid into me easily. I hardly felt it, the coolness of the rubber the only thing letting me know something had been inserted to my ass, but when the second ball entered me, I gasped. Gabriel didn't give me a chance to adjust, the third ball penetrating me until I moaned.

"Beautiful," he said softly, his voice barely more than a whisper. "I really enjoy sticking all sorts of things in my boys' assholes."

Instead of giving me more, he withdrew the dildo. Just when I thought it would leave me, Gabriel thrust it back into me, and I gasped, the sensations strange but good. He fucked me with it, the long, slow motion making me burn, making my cock throb with the need to come. Several times my fingers grasped at the desk, the urge to come drawing my palm to my cock, but I told myself this was not for me, but for Gabriel.

"I'm desperate to feel your ass clench around my cock, Joey. I want to watch as I fuck you for the first time, see the realization cross your face," Gabriel growled. "And yet, I want to savor you, slowly stretch you, so that when I finally do fuck you, you will be mad from pleasure and not pain."

I couldn't respond, my mind a swirl of primal need. I didn't care at this point whether it was the dildo or Gabriel's cock. All I knew was I needed more. As another ball penetrated me, I let go, voicing my shock and pleasure. It was so intense that my palms nearly slid off the polished desk. It was one thing to play with myself in the privacy of my bedroom, but to have this hot, dangerous man pleasuring me? It was the very definition of erotic.

Gabriel got up from his chair, leaving the dildo inside of me.

"Hold it in," he commanded and left the room.

I clenched my muscles, not wanting to disobey. Luckily, he returned quickly.

"Move your hands for a moment," he said and slid a towel under me. "Relax against your elbows."

"Thank you, sir," I said, the position much more comfortable.

Gabriel returned to his seat, his eyes gazing between my legs. He didn't hesitate, coming closer. When the dildo started sliding in and out of me again, I let my head fall back, the pleasure rocketing me off this earth.

"Oh, the fun I'm going to have with you," he murmured. "Start stroking yourself again."

"Yes, sir," I mumbled and gripped my dick. I was so hard, like steel, and it was only a few strokes before the orgasm began to build again. I forced myself to take it slow, to perform for Gabriel, and not try to fulfill my need. He must have liked what he saw, because he growled softly. Then his palm was on my thigh, caressing the skin, cupping my nuts. "Please, sir...."

"You ready to come again, Joey?" he said.

"Yes, sir... please, sir. I need to come so badly," I begged, trying to hold the orgasm at bay.

"Let me see you come," he said. "And make it memorable. If I like what I see then I may have you come often."

I gasped with relief, wanting to thank him, but was unable to speak as the orgasm exploded out of me. He didn't stop pumping my ass with those balls, the sensation heightening the orgasm so that my limbs shook and I could do nothing but voice my pleasure. I felt hot semen splatter across my chest but didn't stop stroking myself, thrusting my hips up into my fist, the experience mind blowing. I thought I might have heard him curse.

When I was able to, I whispered, "Thank you, sir."

When he didn't say anything, I managed to crane my head. He was looking at me like a hunting cat that had just sighted its next meal, his eyes almost glowing with a singular focus. That familiar quirk was back on his lips, and his hand was moving below the desk, as if he were playing with himself.

My lips parted as he pushed the dildo farther into me, the last and largest ball entering me. When it slipped in, my muscles tightened, locking it into place. I moaned softly as he got up, his clothes rasping against the bare skin of my legs. Then he was leaving the room, letting me lay there, nothing more than a puddle on his desk.

He returned quickly, though, and handed me a wet washcloth. "Clean yourself."

"Yes, sir," I muttered, and wiped the cum from my chest.

The dildo was still in me, and I was reminded of that fact every time I moved. When I looked up to him, my eyes immediately fell to the tent in his pants, the outline of his erection vaguely visible. I wanted him in my mouth again, wanted to feel that veiny length stretching my lips and filling my throat... or, if Gabriel preferred, buried deep in my ass.

"Joey?" I could hear the growl in his voice.

When I realized he was speaking to me, I snapped my eyes to his. "Yes, sir?"

He chuckled. "You want your master's cock again?"

I licked my lips hungrily. "Yes, sir... please."

"Come over here and show me how bad you want it," he commanded.

I didn't hesitate, sliding off the desk to kneel in front of him. I automatically gripped my wrists behind my back to keep from reaching for him. As I met the image of his black slacks outlining his erection, I looked up at him.

"Well, what are you waiting for?" he pushed.

I licked my lips and pressed my tongue against Gabriel's erection, running it up and down the length, my saliva soaking into the fabric. I was desperate to get to what lay underneath, desperate to pleasure him, and if this was the only way, then when I was done, his pants would be soaked. Daringly, I dragged my teeth across the fabric, and he hissed, fisting his hand in my hair. He pressed me closer and muttered curses.

"Fucking hell, you try me like no other," he growled.

I found his glans through his pants and sucked at it, eliciting more strangled sounds. His words had given me confidence, and as I pleasured him, I grinned against the fabric. Gabriel yanked my head away, and I looked up at him for direction.

His eyes were intense, his lips tight, but then he grinned wolfishly. "Look what you did, slave."

I glanced at his crotch. The slacks were wet from my efforts. It looked as if he'd spilled a drink in his lap.

Gabriel chuckled. "You want my cock that bad, Joey?"

"Yes, sir!" I didn't hesitate.

"Good boy," he praised, and undid his button and fly. He didn't take his prick out, instead pressing me closer. "You want it? You have to work for it."

I moaned, licking at his shaft, and kissed the ridged skin. I was surprised he wasn't wearing any underwear, but that just left less for me to try to get through. "M-may I touch you, sir?"

"No," he said simply.

I didn't stop licking, tonguing a vein, trying to bide my time. I wasn't sure what to do. I wanted to suck him down, but I couldn't free his dick without touching. An idea popped into my head. I bit into one of the lapels and pulled it away, then used my tongue to try and pull his cock out. I made little progress, but he seemed pleased with my efforts. I tugged more on the pants with my teeth and pushed them away with my cheek until I found his glans. I managed to wiggle him loose using my tongue and a lot of effort until finally his cock popped out.

He laughed, his voice booming. "Good boy. Now take your reward."

I smiled up at him, then kissed his cock head and licked at the bead of precum. I slowly took him into my mouth, trying to be seductive, until he hit the back of my throat. Before I choked, I retreated, kissing the underside of his glans and tonguing the wrinkles. When he gasped, I swallowed him again and sucked him off, sure to hit the underside of his glans with my tongue.

Gabriel muttered curses, his fingers tightening in my hair. I wanted to try and deep-throat him, but he seemed to be liking what I was doing, his breath hitching.

Suddenly, he yanked my head away and growled, "Accept."

I extended my tongue and watched as his expression tightened. He peeled his lips back from his teeth and snarled, and I felt my mouth fill with hot cum. I accepted all that he had to give, getting closer, so close that I sucked at his glans. He didn't seem to mind, huffing and puffing as the orgasm subsided. When he looked back down at me, I stuck my tongue out, and he chuckled.

"Swallow." He gave the command, and I obeyed.

His grip loosened in my hair, and his thumb came around to touch my lip gently.

"Good boy," he whispered.

I couldn't help but smile like an idiot.

Six

TIME HAD passed so quickly. After our session in his office, he had instructed me to clean up, then come downstairs when I was done. I had made sure his desk was sparkling before I was done and that the cleaning supplies were neatly back in their place before I made my way to the first floor. Before I had entered the kitchen, I had slipped into the bathroom, making sure I looked my best for Gabriel. I had swiped a little mouthwash, hoping he didn't mind. I didn't think he would.

When I entered the kitchen, he had called me to him before I could present myself. He had removed the plug from my ass. It had been a relief—every movement I made reminded me of it. He had proceeded to explain to me that it would be my responsibility to clean my toys. My cheeks had heated at that, but I listened carefully as Gabriel went into detail on how I was to do this and informed me I would suffer an instant and harsh punishment should I deviate. Hygiene is important, he had said. I had followed his instructions, located a giant pot like the one Aunt Hanny had used to cook Thanksgiving Day turkeys in, and filled it halfway. I set the plug in and watched as the water came to a slow boil on the stove. Once that was done, I took the pot into the laundry room, where it was emptied and the plug set to dry on a towel. Gabriel had watched me intently, and apparently I had passed. He then sent me into the bathroom to wash my hands.

When I returned, he had explained to me that he enjoyed cooking and running the show and that I was to be his "little helper." He had me retrieving ingredients for him and chopping up cucumbers and tomatoes. He made Caesar salad with chicken for us, and as I set the table for him, he had quickly corrected me.

"You will eat with your master, but you should make sure that I have everything I need before sitting down to eat yourself," he said, his attention on assembling the salad. "Pour me a glass of iced tea and use the rest of the lemon you mangled earlier. Place it next to my setting."

"Yes, sir," I confirmed, and set myself a place setting, then poured him his drink, squeezing the lemons into the tea. I had to wash my hands again, my fingers wet with lemon juice. I made a mental note to buy some lemons and practice cutting them at home.

When everything was done, he set two plates on the table and took his seat.

"Do you need anything else, sir?" I inquired.

"No, I'm good," he said and took a sip of his tea.

I sat down at my end of the table, trying to be quiet. After a few minutes of forks clanking, I said, "Thank you, sir. For the food."

He nodded, chewing his meal. When he was able, he spoke. "A good master takes care of his slave. Some masters like to use food and bathroom rights against their slaves, but I want to remind you that that won't happen here."

"Thank you, sir," I said, feeling relieved. Throughout this whole thing, my biggest fear was being relegated an *It*. Maybe that did it for some people, but not me.

"Eat your food." He pointed at my hardly touched plate.

"Yes, sir." I still didn't feel all that hungry, but I forced myself to eat—after all, Gabriel had worked so hard to make the dish for me—and it was delicious, the chicken perfectly cooked and seasoned.

"This is really good, sir," I praised.

He seemed delighted that his hard work was appreciated. "I'm glad you approve. Should you sign a contract with me, you should know that you will be my test dummy for new recipes."

I beamed at him, happy to be of service.

"Do you have any questions, Joey?" he inquired.

"Ah…." I wanted to ask more about him but wasn't sure how to broach the subject.

"Do not be afraid to ask me something. If I don't want to talk about it, I will simply let you know. You will come to learn that I am very vocal, and it's important to talk about what is happening between us," he said, his eyes piercing me. "Communication is vital."

I took a deep breath and parted my lips. "I was just wondering… if you'd tell me more about… you. I mean, like where you grew up and stuff?"

"That's good, Joey. It's important that we know each other well if you are interested in pursuing a more… *permanent* position with me." He smiled, taking a sip of his tea. "As I've told you before, I spent most of my childhood years in a small town called New Mill just north of the Illinois-Wisconsin border. It is mainly an industrial town, but the years have been hard, a lot of the factories closing. However, there is a small sector on the eastern border—the locals call it Green-miles—green as in money. My family came from 'old money,' as some men might call it, migrating to the States in the early nineteen hundreds to expand their shipping business into the Americas."

"You're European, then?" I asked.

He nodded. "My mother was a full-blooded Brit, my father French. They met when my father was in the UK on a business trip. So I'm told, anyway. I've heard that we have a lot of political activists in the family, stretching back a few hundred years. I guess it's in my blood to be critical of today's politics."

I smiled—no wonder he was so damned sexy. "Can you speak French?"

"*Oui*," he said, then went on to speak fluently, an accent coming through.

I had no idea what he said, but judging from the wicked smirk, it was something naughty. I blushed and wet my throat with some water.

"What about you, Joey? Have any family history?" he inquired.

I shrugged, wishing I had a story to tell. "Aunt Hanny has told me my grandfather was half Italian and German, but beyond that, I really don't know. I have no idea who my father is, so… yeah."

"Have you ever tried to find him?" Gabriel inquired.

I shrugged. "Not really." I hadn't even known where to look.

He nodded, finishing off his salad. "I grew up around the factories but never really took an interest in the business. I figured my father already had his heir to the throne, so I decided to pursue other avenues."

"You have brothers and sisters, then?" I asked.

"An older brother, yes." He shrugged, then nodded to my empty plate. "Good?"

"Yes, thank you, sir." I hadn't realized I had finished it all, but now that I'd eaten, I felt better. "So why did you decide to be a… money manager? I mean, when I was a kid I always dreamed of being weird, unproductive things. Even now, I guess I've sort of followed that dream, but—I don't know. No offense, but it seems like such a mundane thing."

He laughed softly and sat back in his chair. "I ended up going to business school no matter how determined I was to rebel against my father. I guess I wanted to prove that hard work trumped inheritance. My father is a CEO of the shipping company, and I guess I wanted to separate myself from that inheritance. Not that there is anything wrong with it, but everything I own has come from my hard work, and that fills me with pride. You can't get that when everything is handed to you."

I nodded, not completely understanding. Maybe it was just that I came from a modest background, but Gabriel seemed proud that he'd made his own way. It wasn't that I was lazy—Hanny and I had had to work hard for what little we had—but I thought it might be nice to not have to fight for everything. I guess I was a little jaded.

"Well." He patted his belly. "That was good."

"It was. Thank you, sir." I smiled. "Should I collect the plates?"

"Yes," he said simply and finished off his iced tea.

I got up and gathered the plates and silverware and dumped them into the sink.

"Make sure the dishes are free of debris, then put them into the washer and turn it on. I've already loaded it with soap. When you are done, come into the living room," he ordered.

"Yes, sir," I confirmed, and turned the water on.

I felt him pass me, that brush of his dark cologne penetrating me. I hurried up with my chore, determined to join him, but was sure to do everything to perfection so he could not find fault. I wiped the table and counter down for good measure and set the washcloth over the sink faucet. I took a few moments for myself, then entered the living room quietly, presenting myself to him. He was reading a newspaper, elegant glasses framing his face.

He didn't look away from the paper as he spoke. "Come closer."

I obeyed, scooting across the carpet to join him at his feet. He didn't say anything further, just touched me softly on my shoulder. I sighed at the touch and listened as he whispered curses at the articles.

"Here," he said, handing me the remote. "Feel free to watch television."

"Thank you, sir," I said, and flipped through the channels, not finding much that kept my interest despite the hundreds of different options. It was comforting, being so close to Gabriel, relaxing and enjoying the evening. The sound of paper crunching soothed me, and as he pulled me closer to him, the warmth of his body comforted me.

"Are you cold?" he inquired.

"No, sir, it's actually comfortable."

"Let me know if you get cold," he ordered.

"Yes, sir," I confirmed, and went back to surfing the channels. I wasn't sure how much time had passed, the sky outside getting darker and darker. I heard the newspaper rustle behind me before he sighed. Fingers dug into my hair, stroking me softly—I thought I might have moaned.

"Come up here," he said, his tone soft.

I obeyed, climbing onto the couch. He pulled me in, wrapping an arm around my shoulders, and I settled my head on his chest. This felt so much better, and I was glad he had given me this opportunity. I whispered a "Thank you, sir." His thumb stroked my bare arm, that touch sending shivers up my spine. I wasn't sure how long I lay like that, but I felt my lids grow heavy, my breath even out, and—

"Joey?"

I snapped awake. "Yes, sir?"

He chuckled. "Looks like I lost you. It's been a busy day for you, hasn't it?"

"Yes, sir, sorry, sir," I mumbled.

"Come on." He patted my ass. "It's late, and I'm tired too."

I followed him up the stairs, unable to keep myself from yawning. He led me into his bedroom, and I gaped. It was huge, a giant bed covered in black silk sheets set against the wall. Though it was extravagant, it was also neat, with everything in its place. There were double doors that led out onto a balcony. I watched as Gabriel peeled the sheet back, then undid his shirt.

"You will always sleep with me so that if I need something during the night, you will be available immediately," he explained.

"Whether it be a drink of water or a blow job, it will be your duty to fulfill my request. Do you understand?"

"Yes, sir," I confirmed and watched as he undressed.

He had a wonderful back, strong, the muscles defined, and as he slid his pants down, my jaw nearly dislodged. He had a gorgeous ass. I could just picture my fingers digging into it as he fucked me— if he would allow me to touch him, anyhow. I watched with longing eyes as he strutted past me and disappeared through a door. I heard running water, a swishing that sounded like teeth being brushed. I waited… heard the swoosh of a toilet flushing.

Gabriel emerged from the bathroom and said, "If you need to use the bathroom, do so now. In the linen closet, you will find a brand new toothbrush and tube of toothpaste. Feel free to use them."

"Thank you, sir," I murmured and took the opportunity.

Whoa. His private bathroom was even bigger than the one downstairs, and wow, he had a hot tub. I grinned. I'd never lived in such elegance before, even if I was a temporary houseguest. I relieved myself, then located the toothbrush and paste. I discarded the packaging and scrubbed my teeth. I was hoping he might kiss me tonight, just once. I wanted to know what his lips felt like against mine.

When I exited the bathroom and saw Gabriel sitting up in his bed, I thought this was the first time I was going to sleep with another man. Sure, I'd spent some time in a bed before, but it had only been for an hour for the exchange of blow jobs, and then I was sent on my merry way. But to actually sleep? This was all new to me. Oh God… what if I farted in my sleep?

"Joey?" Gabriel prompted.

"Huh?" I blinked at him. "I mean, yes, sir?"

He patted the space next to him.

"Yes, sir," I mumbled, and came around to the other side.

I got in gingerly, trying to be quiet, though I had no idea why. I lay down, facing him but on the edge, scared to take up too much space. He flipped the sheets over us, then turned around and reached for the light.

I parted my lips, wanting to speak, feeling like a child. The room went dark, and I swallowed hard. It was fine, really. I was in a big, soft bed, in a huge-ass bedroom with a sexy man next to me. The door was right behind me, and I could walk out if I needed to. There was nothing to be afraid of. Of course, my brain thought otherwise. I felt the panic hit me, and I closed my eyes, trying to concentrate on relaxing.

I felt Gabriel get closer, the bed dipping from his weight, and an arm came around me, pulling me to him. I gasped, but not from his touch as he must have thought, but because it had suddenly become hard to breathe. I felt cold, weak....

"Joey? Is everything okay?" he inquired, his tone suspicious.

"I'm sorry, sir... I ah, I'm nyctophobic." I swallowed. "Scared of the... dark."

I heard him whisper a curse, and the bed shifted again. The room quickly filled with light. My brain seemed to remember how to work my lungs, and I took a deep breath, but when I saw the look on Gabriel's face, I stilled.

He got out of bed and slipped his pants on. "My office. Now."

Before I could speak, he was out of the room. I touched my feet to the carpet, my heart banging against my chest. I figured I better not make him wait and forced myself toward his office. When I entered, he was sitting at his desk, the chair facing the window. I made a motion to present, but he pointed at the couch.

"Sit." The word was harsh, angry.

I plopped my butt in the seat, feeling tiny. Gabriel was furious, but I didn't understand why. Oh God, this was why I hadn't wanted to mention it earlier—scared of the dark. It was so childish, and I felt like an idiot admitting to such a thing.

"I had asked you if there was anything that scared you, anything that I needed to know—you said no," he said evenly, still looking out the window. I didn't answer, and when he swiveled his chair around, his gaze was penetrating. "You lied to me—"

"Sir, I—"

His fist slammed on the desk, and I jumped. "Do not interrupt me."

I looked down in shame.

"You have committed an inexcusable offense. In everyday life it might be okay to tell little lies, omit things here and there, but not *here*," he growled. "The only way this works is if you are 100 percent honest. I thought you understood this."

When he didn't say anything else, I opened my mouth. "I thought you would think I was silly. I thought if I'd told you would think I was just some kid."

Gabriel scrubbed his face, then tipped his head back. "Maybe this is partly my fault. You are new to the lifestyle, and I didn't completely inform you of the consequences of omitting said 'silly' things."

I opened my mouth to respond, but he shot out of his chair and stormed for the door. "Come with me."

I obeyed, following, feeling cold in my nakedness, though the temperature was comfortable. He led me down to the first floor and made for the laundry room, but before he would have entered, burst through a door that I assumed led to the basement. I followed him down, the room dim, and—

Gabriel flipped a switch, flooding the basement with light, and I gasped. It was like an underground torture chamber, with shackles hanging on the brick walls. A half-dozen different contraptions occupied the space, some with leather handcuffs attached and... things I had no names for, things I couldn't comprehend, but they frightened me nonetheless.

He wrapped a warm arm around my waist and urged me over to one. I knew what it was—St. Andrew's Cross, bindings hanging from the top for wrists and anklets on the bottom. He pressed me against it, the padded leather cool and soft against the skin of my back. I searched his face for explanation. Thankfully, he didn't shackle me, instead reached to the side and presented me with some sort of leather mask. There were no slits for the eyes, only a small tube to breathe out of. I began to shake in my skin, my bones rattling.

"I rarely ever use this stuff. I guess you could say it's my… symbol of aspiration. You see, I've never gotten to that point where my slave so completely trusts me he is willing to allow me to do *anything*, believing that I will never hurt him, that I hold his safety in the highest regard, trusting me unconditionally," he said, and fingered the mask, as if imagining such a thing. His attention quickly turned toward me. "You might decide you want a contract with me. Maybe one day we might reach that place when you trust me completely. What do you think might have happened if your 'silly' problem slipped through? What would have happened should I have bound you, blind you? Answer the question, Joey."

A glanced at the eyeless mask, fearing it. I swallowed, my mouth dry. I wasn't sure what disappointed me the most—possibly never being able to give Gabriel that or lying about my seemingly inconsequential phobia. "I probably would have had a panic attack."

Gabriel nodded and pressed his body against mine, his hand wrapping around my throat. He forced me to look up at him, and I searched those silver eyes for guidance. "Imagine yourself completely bound, unable to move, unable to see and speak. I'm standing over you, with the misconception that nothing I am about to do could harm you—because you trust me, because I would see you safe. And then that fear sets in. You know it best; you've lived with it. What if something goes wrong? What if I fail to notice right away what's happening? What if I can't free you soon enough?"

As he spoke the words, tears pooled in the corners of my eyes. When I had omitted the truth, I hadn't thought past my own selfish need to be accepted by this man. I didn't think how it might affect him or the things he wanted to do with me.

"I'm so sorry, sir," I muttered.

He let a breath out and stepped away, letting the mask fall to the ground with a thunk. He didn't say anything as he led me back up the stairs and closed the door to the basement. Then we were headed back to his office, the silence loud. He made right for the chair where I had folded my clothes and tossed them at me.

"Get dressed," he ordered, taking his seat at his desk, and proceeded to stare out at the night.

My heart crashed against something painful. I'd blown it. I'd screwed up, and now he was getting rid of me. As I slipped into my pants, I refused to cry—I would not make myself out a child. It wasn't until I tugged my shirt on that he wheeled around to regard me. I was unable to read that expression, his eyes startling me until I looked away.

"We have a very important decision to make, Joey," he said evenly. "My first instinct is to end this. But I have to remind myself that the fault isn't entirely yours. Therefore, I propose an extension to our deal. One more weekend."

I gasped and nodded. "Yes, sir, please! I promise I won't withhold anything ever again. I was just… I don't know. Honestly, this is all very overwhelming, but I do want it. Please, sir, give me another chance."

Gabriel seemed satisfied with my words, his body relaxing. "I'm going to take you home, and you're going to think long and hard on what just happened these next few days. When you come back to me Friday, you will hand me an essay—no less than five hundred words on why it was wrong to omit the truth and why I should give you another chance. I swear, for every word under, you will receive five points added to your tally. It will be double-spaced and handwritten or typed, I don't care which. In addition, you have automatically earned two hundred points, which means you have two punishments coming next week, so be prepared when you arrive here. Do not expect me to be lenient in dealing out said punishment. Do you still wish to extend our deal?"

I didn't hesitate. "Yes, sir! Thank you, sir!"

He said no more and got up, disappearing from his office. I could do nothing but stand there, my breath uneven. I couldn't believe he was giving me another chance. When he returned, he was dressed.

"Let's go," he ordered.

I followed. I wanted to stay with him, make it up to him, but maybe I really needed to sit down and think about this. Yes, I had enjoyed what time I had spent with him, but it had been startling at the same time. On some level, I couldn't believe it was a part of me, that I was willing to serve another in all ways—serve in the manner of a *sex slave*. That title still wasn't comfortable on my lips.

The drive home was silent. Once we got off the Stevenson Expressway, Gabriel had requested directions to my house again. I obliged and apologized for making him drive all the way out here. He didn't respond to that. When we got to my house, I sighed, wanting the night to end, to go on. I didn't want to leave him, and yet I wanted some private time.

"Remember what I said. Five hundred words, double-spaced, written or typed. I will call you later this week to confirm your arrival."

"Yes, sir," I mumbled, then got out of the car. As soon as I closed the door, he sped off. I watched as his car disappeared around the corner, digging up debris and dust. I must have stood there a good half hour, but eventually I made it into the house.

Aunt Hanny was asleep, so I made sure to be quiet as I entered my room. I flipped the light switch and collapsed in my bed.

I cried myself to sleep, hating every tear.

Seven

FRIDAY HAD come sooner than expected.

Sunday had been hell for me, and I had spent most of the day in my room under the excuse that I had a bad migraine. Aunt Hanny had been sweet, trying to wait on me, but I had wished she'd just leave me alone. Monday had been better, Gabriel leaving me a text message to let me know what he expected of me come Friday and where and what time he'd pick me up. I had wanted to call him but was afraid I'd make the situation worse.

Knowing that he was still interested in me managed to perk me up just a little. The essay he had demanded had been heavy on my mind. It seemed silly to me, having to write an essay like a schoolkid. It wasn't until Wednesday when I realized that was the point. I had to admit to myself that I had handled the whole thing rather immaturely. Instead of being honest and confessing to my phobia like an adult, I had hidden in hope of being accepted, like a child. I still blamed my rough childhood for that one, but I needed to get past it.

So, now that Friday had come at me from out of nowhere, I was left sitting at my sluggish computer at one o'clock in the afternoon, the cursor blinking at me. I hadn't written a thing, my mind blank. Time was ticking away, and I still needed to prepare myself for Gabriel. But this was important, and for the first time in a long time, I had no idea how to express myself. Words had always

99

been my solace. When I was unable to speak my feelings, I poured my emotions into poems and English-class assignments.

I decided to at least start with the punishment itself. I detailed how I had originally thought that writing an essay was silly, but that I now understood the point of it. Once I got that out of the way, the words just started flowing, and before I knew it, I was finished. I read it several times over, perfecting the flow, trying to get all my feelings down in coherent sentences. It was three by the time I printed it.

It was as good as I was going to get it, so I set it on my bed, then collected the clothes I had prepared to wear this evening. If I were lucky, I wouldn't be dressed for very long. I stopped downstairs to get a quick drink and found Aunt Hanny getting ready to leave for her Friday social outing with some friends.

"Hey, baby." She smiled. "I put some meatloaf and potatoes in the fridge if you're hungry. I'll probably be home late tonight."

I nodded. "Yeah, I might not be home at all."

"Oh? Another school function?"

"Something like that." I smiled tightly and kissed her on the cheek. I dug in the fridge and found the orange juice.

"Is everything okay, Joey?" she inquired. "You've been acting strange these past few weeks.

I leaned against the counter and shrugged. I would consider myself one foot out of the closet. I didn't hide the fact that I was gay, but I didn't flaunt it either. I'd never told Aunt Hanny, more from lack of opportunity than anything. I'd never had a committed boyfriend in high school, so she never asked whom I spent my time with because I was always home. It was just something that I hadn't gotten around to, so it felt unusual that I really wanted to tell her now.

"No, I'm fine. Just worried about school," I said. It was a half-truth. *Coward*, I told myself. I guess I was afraid of our relationship changing should it be revealed. Not to mention, what would she think of me if she knew I liked being ordered around and "used" in ways she couldn't even imagine?

"Okay, well, call me and let me know you're okay."

"I will. Have fun, Auntie," I said, and accepted another kiss on the cheek.

When she was gone and I'd had my fill of OJ, I ran upstairs and ran some hot water in the sink. I had decided to tackle my chest first before moving on to other areas. I lathered up my chest with shaving cream, feeling weird. I was careful with the razor, afraid I'd cut myself.

I ended up going through three razors as I stripped my chest, butt cheeks, underarms, and pubic region. I was sure I had gotten it all. I could safely say I now knew how women felt. I stepped into the shower, scrubbing my hair and my body raw, wanting to be perfect for Gabriel. By the time I was done, my body was flushed from heat and my auntie's abrasive scrubber, but I looked good. My skin was slick from the water and looked so smooth with no hair. I didn't look too bad. I just hoped I pleased Gabriel tonight.

I burst into my room, drying my hair, and stepped into my new-old jeans, figuring I'd have no use for boxers. My simple black long sleeve was next. The clothes felt weird against my shaved skin, as if the cloth was heavier. I only had a half hour until I needed to hop on the bus, so I brushed my teeth and styled my hair the best I could. It usually did its own thing, anyway.

I was such a frazzled mess as I rushed to get everything together that I nearly forgot my essay. I stuck it in my backpack neatly and took a last look in the mirror. I took a deep breath and slowly let it out. When I was ready, I headed out the door and plopped down on the bench by the bus stop. I'd be lying if I said I wasn't nervous, scared, confused, but I wanted this, I wanted Gabriel to give me another chance.

I didn't have to wait long for the bus. "Well, well, Mr. Mantello. It's been a while."

"Hello, Mr. Frazier." I smiled. I'd known Mr. Frazier for years, since the first day of high school. He'd been the first to speak up for me against the bullies, making them sit at the back of the bus and me right behind him. He had meant well, but his deeds usually made everything worse when there were no adults around to protect me. Still, I had enjoyed talking to him. He had told me his son had died a few years ago in the war and had wanted to be a writer just like me.

"Look at you. Have a date?" He winked.

I blushed. "Something like that, sir."

"Lucky girl."

"Yeah." It was funny the way people always assumed you were heterosexual, but I didn't question it. I mean, the man had to have heard the bullies' anti-gay slurs thrown at me. Maybe it was just his way of letting me know he didn't care about my orientation. Maybe one day I'd ask.

"Well, good luck, handsome."

"Thanks."

I took my seat at the back, wanting some privacy, and bumped my head against the glass. I closed my eyes. I had imagined a million scenarios in what direction tonight might take, and all of them were uncertain. After reading my essay, Gabriel might very well decide I was not worth his effort. I would be crushed, and what little self-confidence I had would die a slow, painful death. It wouldn't be the end of the world, though. I had promised myself I would take everything that happened as a learning experience.

Think positive, I told myself. The rocking motion of the bus actually soothed me, and I relaxed, falling into a half-sleeplike state. I could still hear the murmur of conversations, the driver calling out the stops. When I heard him call the Midway station, I flipped my eyes open. I took a cleansing breath and got up. I exited and immediately found Gabriel's Camaro.

My heart started pounding as I headed toward the car. My hand was shaky as I pulled on the door handle and slipped in quietly.

I supposed him being here at all was a good sign. If he was willing to drive halfway across the city, then there must be a worthwhile reason to do so.

Gabriel was relaxing, his head back against the seat. His shades were on, so I couldn't tell if his eyes were closed, but he spoke. "How are you, Joey?"

"Ah, o-okay…," I stuttered. "You, sir?"

"Same ole," he said. "You have everything with you?"

"Yes, sir." I knew he had meant the essay.

He didn't say anything else. He started the car, the engine roaring to life, and bolted out of the station. When we got on the expressway, he zoomed into the fast lane, and it felt as if we were flying. He had to be doing ninety, and I wondered how many speeding tickets he had to his name. Unfortunately, we ran into traffic, and Gabriel was forced to take it below sixty. He muttered curses at the cars.

"How was work?" I inquired, the silence deafening to me.

"Fucking fantastic," he growled, not at all pleased. "Son-of-a-bitch Riley pisses me off like no other. The man needs to go."

I was glad to know there was another that had upset him more than I had. He went on a little more about the man's incompetence, snarling and snapping as we weaved in and out of traffic. When we got off the expressway and headed into his community, my stomach started tumbling. I was glad I had passed on the meatloaf.

Every step up to his house was hard, my legs feeling heavy. I slipped my shoes off in the hallway, waiting for him as he did the same. I followed him up the stairs. His office seemed too far, yet it was only a few feet away. I closed the door behind me and watched as he shrugged out of his jacket and hung it on the hook, his shoulders rolling under his dress shirt. He took a seat at his desk and leaned back, his shades coming off in slow motion. Those quicksilver eyes ran up and down my body before settling on my face.

He pointed at the chair next to the desk. "Clothes. Off."

"Yes, sir," I muttered and set my bag down. I stripped quickly, not wanting to make him wait. I folded my stuff neatly and set it on the chair. I made a motion to present, but he stopped me.

"You have something for me?" he asked simply.

"Yes, sir." I dug the essay out of my backpack and straightened the paper. I set it on his desk in front of him.

He cocked his head, his eyes on the paper, but he didn't take it. "Printed, double-spaced."

He got up and moved to the corner, where I noticed a video camera was mounted. "I always record my boys' punishments and will not be making an exception with you. Once this weekend is out and you decide to move on, it will be destroyed."

"Yes, sir," I said weakly.

He came to sit on the couch, stretching his arms along the back. "Read it."

I swallowed and fetched the paper, then stood in the middle of the room feeling... well, naked. I cleared my throat and started reading, but I couldn't catch my breath. I stumbled over several words, my cheeks heating. I'd never had a problem speaking in public before, so I didn't understand how Gabriel could startle me so much that I couldn't speak in front of one person.

"Joey."

I looked at him hopelessly. "Yes, sir?"

"Close your eyes and take a deep breath," he said, and I obeyed. "Now let it out slowly. Good, again."

Several breaths later and I stopped shaking, his guidance soothing me.

"Better?"

"Yes, sir, thank you, sir," I said, licking my lips. When he nodded, I started reading from the beginning.

Dear Master Gabriel,

I didn't start writing until this afternoon, unable to collect my thoughts, but I had thought long and hard about what had happened. I've never before struggled with putting my voice on the page, and I know it is because my actions truly rattled me. I realize now the severity of my behavior.

In the beginning, I couldn't understand why you wanted me to write an essay—it seemed so silly, immature, like a school assignment. Then I understood. My actions in lying to you were immature and childish, and this punishment suddenly seemed fitting.

When I had omitted my phobia, it was because I wanted you to accept me. I felt that if I had disclosed my fear, you would see me as a curious boy rather than a serious man. I realize now that by lying about it, I had done that exact thing. You have no idea how much I regret that decision, and it in no way excuses my behavior. More importantly, though, I disappointed you and potentially put myself at risk. I did not think past my own selfish desires, and in doing so, completely missed the point of submitting to you.

I did not look past what I had wanted, did not trust you to accept me as I am. I did not think about future consequences. All I could see was my own endgame. I have thought about what you had shown me in the basement, and I realize now I had jeopardized my safety. I did not think about how you might have felt should I have been injured. I didn't see past my own wants that it would have shattered your trust in me.

I don't think I've ever truly known what it is to trust someone. Through no fault of her own, my mom abandoned me at an early age. I never knew my father. A friend locked me in a dark place for fun. I was never the popular kid in school, shunned because I didn't belong. The only one I've ever had is my aunt, and sometimes I can't help but think she feels obligated to look after me.

This is perhaps one of the hardest things I've had to write, but I truly want to be honest with you. You scare me, but I want to be the best I can be for you. You have given me the opportunity to explore those feelings I thought were wrong, were the reason I was labeled a freak. You came into my life and showed me that there are people who think otherwise, who would accept me. You are one of those people, and I am so sorry I lied to you, gave you a reason to distrust me.

I realize that I've also lied to myself.

I don't deserve a second chance. Not in something like this. It's too important, too serious. But I still ask you to give me one, beg you to let me try again. I really want this, but I don't yet understand just how significant it is, how big a part of me it is. It frightens me. I hope you can extend a little trust to me again, and in turn I promise to give you all of me.

I'm so sorry.

Sincerely,

Joey Mantello

I couldn't believe I'd gotten that all out. Tears had pooled in the corners of my eyes, and I wasn't sure why. I guess really talking about my feelings had released pent-up frustration. While tormented in high school, I had always kept it to myself, because I didn't want to tell Aunt Hanny her "golden boy" was a loser. As the last words left me, I looked down, too scared to see the expression on Gabriel's face. He was quiet for several moments. I was sure I didn't want to know what he was thinking.

His voice startled me like a loud noise in a quiet room. "Why are you afraid of the dark, Joey?"

I swallowed hard, totally expecting the question, but that didn't make it any easier to answer. "A boy locked me in a toy box when I was three. I couldn't get out, couldn't see anything. I wasn't found for hours. I developed night terrors, but I'm okay now. It's just dark rooms that get to me. I usually need a small light on. I guess the darkness just reminds me of the toy box."

"I am diabetic. Did you know that?" he said.

I nodded. "I had seen that in your medical report."

"Do you think I chose to be?" he inquired, his tone even, warm. "Did you choose for that little bastard to lock you in there and leave?"

My attention snapped to him, and I searched his handsome face. He didn't look mad, his expression as relaxed as his body was. I shook my head. "No, sir."

"Come sit down." He motioned to the empty spot next to him. "Leave the essay on my desk. I will be checking the word count later."

I smiled shyly and set the paper on his desk, then came to join him on the couch. I couldn't get comfortable, the leather cool against my skin, Gabriel's intense gaze hot on me.

"Do you hold my diabetic status against me?" he inquired. "Do you think it makes me a lesser man?"

I looked around the room, as if the furniture could offer me advice. "No, of course not, sir."

"Then what makes you think I would hold your phobia against you?"

My jaw fell open as I looked at him. I could not answer. I shook my head at my own idiocy. "I suppose I got so used to sticking to myself when I was a kid, that it's affecting me still."

Gabriel nodded. "That is understandable. Just to clarify, I do not think there is something wrong with you or see you as a frightened child. Do you want to know what I see, Joey?"

I looked into his eyes, the silver nearly glowing. "Yes, sir."

"I see a handsome young man coming into his own and discovering his sexuality for the first time," he said, his words reaching deep inside of me. "It might be frightening, but you have to embrace it, reach for it. It is who you are, and it is nothing to be ashamed of."

My eyes had nearly popped out of my skull. All I could do was look at this man, this sexy, powerful man who had all his shit together, knew what and who he was. I managed a nod. I wondered if he had gone through the same thing when he was a kid, confused by his private thoughts.

"Come here," he said, and I scooted closer. He scooped me into his arms, and I moaned at the contact, needing it desperately. "I know this is a confusing time. Not only are you unfamiliar with your sexuality, but you are still young, caught up by the thinking of a teenager. You need to take time to think about things—not just about this, but life in general. Acting on impulse isn't productive."

"Thank you, sir," I whispered against his shirt. I swore if I listened closely, I could hear his heart beat.

"I'm willing to give you another chance, Joey," Gabriel said against my hair. "But you have got to be honest with me in everything, even if something seems silly or inconsequential. It's imperative that you trust me."

"Yes, sir, thank you, sir." I felt the tears prick my eyes again. "I swear I will not lie to you again."

"I believe you," he said. "Now, before we go any further, is there anything else you might want to tell me?"

I blushed and looked up at him. Meekly, I admitted, "I don't like spiders."

He laughed, his voice a smooth curl. "I don't much like them either."

I couldn't help but smile.

"Feel better?" he asked.

I sighed with relief. "Yes, sir."

"Good. Because it's time to talk about your punishment now. For the first one hundred points, I assigned you the essay, and I am satisfied it had the effect I had intended. But you are still due another," he said, his voice going a little dark.

I nodded. "I understand, sir."

He got up and left the room. I sat there, blown away by everything that had happened. On some level I was glad, for it had brought me closer to my desires and perhaps to Gabriel, though it wasn't easy admitting to my fears. Still, it made me hopeful. And Gabriel had given me another chance.

When he returned, he was carrying a towel and a small bottle of oil, but what caught my attention was the wooden paddle. I swallowed hard as he set it on the table next to him, then came to join me on the couch.

"Get your book," he ordered.

"Yes, sir," I croaked, and retrieved it from the table.

"Open it."

I did as instructed and spotted his handwriting. He had given me two hundred points for lying to him about my phobia. I knew it was well earned.

"Add up the total of infractions incurred during the week. Then deduct two hundred." I did as he commanded, and I was left with forty points, which meant if I wanted to avoid a punishment next weekend, I was only allowed sixty points. If we signed a contract, anyhow. When I was done, I returned the book to the table.

"You understand why I am administering punishment, then. Do you have any questions?"

I took a deep breath and shook my head in agreement. I was ready to accept it.

I watched out of the corner of my eye as he laid the towel over his lap.

"Come here. Bend over my knees."

I reluctantly obeyed, letting him guide me into the correct position. My ass was over his thighs, my legs on the couch. He gave me a leather pillow to use, and I forced myself to relax. I was actually fairly comfortable, and when Gabriel stroked my ass, I sighed.

"Why am I punishing you, Joey?" he inquired.

"For lying to you, sir." I didn't hesitate.

"I'm going to spank you now. Do not attempt to wiggle away or prevent the blows," he ordered, his tone strict. "To do so will earn you additional lashes. I also want you to remember that your safeword is available for use. Do you understand?"

I swallowed hard. "Yes, sir."

I couldn't deny the sense of eroticism his words brought. Though I knew this probably wasn't going to turn out good for me, my dick hardened a little. Maybe it was just the rough texture of the towel or Gabriel's warm palms on my ass. I jerked as the first slap hit me, the sound loud and shocking. Gabriel issued a constant stream of spanks, each alternating between my cheeks. I rested my head against the pillow.

The sensation quickly lit me up, arousing me, but that passed swiftly, and it wasn't long before I was hissing. My ass had begun to feel hot, each spank seeming to get harder and harder until I moaned in discomfort. I tried to take deep breaths as the ache morphed into the beginnings of pain. Gabriel didn't give me a break, his heavy palm assaulting my ass over and over until I whimpered and rocked my hips in an effort to stem the pain.

It felt as if I'd sat on the hot summer pavement naked, the heat uncomfortable, the surface abrasive. I wished he would give me a few seconds to collect myself, but he was merciless. The first sob was wretched from my lips, and my eyes burned as my ass was lit on fire. My body protested, and I kicked the couch in search of relief, but I got none.

"Not fun, is it?" Gabriel asked.

"No, sir!" I whimpered, giving it my all to stay right where I was. I wanted to stay here, bent over his knee to receive my punishment, but my body had other ideas.

Gabriel stopped the spanking, and I moaned in relief, the sting easing just a little. But then there was something cool and hard pressed against my sore flesh. I knew what it was, and I couldn't help but sob.

"Do you remember what I told you about counting out the spanks issued with anything other than my hand?" Gabriel asked.

I sniffled. "Yes, sir."

The whack of the paddle startled me, the slap filling the room. I barked, shocked by the pain. "One, sir!"

Gabriel didn't let up, and though the spanks were spaced a little more, the pain was a lot more intense. By the tenth paddle I could barely speak, my voice hoarse as I struggled to count them. A tear escaped, and I made a motion to wipe it away, but Gabriel gripped my wrist.

"No. Your tears belong to me. Do not try to hide them," he said harshly.

When the fifteenth spank came, I was sobbing like a child, my face wet with tears. My ass was hot and felt swollen, the sting encompassing my entire backside.

"Do you think you've had enough? Have you learned your lesson, Joey?" Gabriel inquired. "If you can't take it, then use your safeword."

Yes, yes, yes, please.... I wanted to beg him to stop, but.... "No, sir. Please... more, sir...."

The paddle met my ass again, and I jerked, punching the couch. "Sixteen, sir!"

The twentieth spank was the hardest, and my cries bounced off the wall. I wouldn't be surprised if the neighbors heard me. Gabriel's palm on my behind startled me, and his normally smooth skin felt like sandpaper against my spanked bottom. I moaned as he stroked me, my chin trembling. I didn't think I could take any more, not without thrashing and fighting him. I didn't want to do that. I wanted to accept it for him.

"Good boy," he praised. "Come here."

My body was like rubber as I lifted myself off his knees. He guided me to him, wrapping me up in his arms, my ass between his legs—the leather was cold and welcomed against my behind. When I was settled, I looked up into his face, his expression remarkably kind. He ran his fingers through my hair, then wiped my tears away.

"I'm proud that you've accepted your punishment without fuss," he said, and my insides jumped. "Penance has been paid, and we will put your transgression behind us. Yes?"

I nodded and said weakly, "Yes, sir."

"Good boy," he whispered, and I relaxed in his arms. "You will not dwell on it, and I will never bring it up again. It is behind us now, and we will look to the future. You're going to feel the results of your punishment for the next few days, but when you think of it, I want you to think of this moment. I want you to know that all sin has been washed away. Do you understand what I am telling you?"

"Yes, sir. I... do." I nodded, committing his face to memory. I'd seen amused Gabriel and even furious Gabriel, but this gentle Gabriel was new to me.

He kissed me on the forehead and praised me more, and tears came to my eyes again, but they were happy tears. I was so relieved that I had been able to make amends. "Thank you, sir."

I wasn't sure how long I lay in his arms, his voice comforting like a lullaby, his body warm and solid. Remarkably, as my tears dried and my body calmed, I felt better despite the ache in my ass, felt as if I had been cleansed. It was weird, but I didn't question it.

"Come, bend over the couch," Gabriel said. He must have seen my stricken expression, because he went on, "Your punishment is over, Joey. I need to take care of you."

I swallowed hard but did as told, my body heavy as I bent over the couch and exposed my ass. I heard something click. Then the light scent of almond filled my nostrils. I gasped as Gabriel rubbed something cool and moist on my ass.

"Almond oil with aloe, it will protect your skin," he explained, his touch gentle.

I moaned, the sensation feeling both good and bad, soothing yet irritating. I was glad that he was so concerned with my health. It made me feel important, cherished. I now truly understood his position. Safety was first and foremost, and I had put him in a bad situation by lying. When he was done, he pulled me against him, wrapping his arm around my torso. His free hand guided my hand to his arm, allowing me to touch him, and I fell into him. Gabriel pressed a kiss against my neck.

"Do you have any questions or concerns about what just happened?" he asked. "You can tell me anything. I want you to express your feelings."

I took a moment to think about what I had just experienced. "I'm just glad I was able to make it right, sir."

"Good." He smiled. "It's late, I'm tired, and we have a busy day ahead of us tomorrow. We will be resuming training, and I want you well rested."

He turned off the recorder, then took my hand and led me out of the office and into his bedroom.

"Go use the bathroom. Get ready for bed," he instructed.

"Yes, sir," I said and closed the bathroom door behind me.

I took a moment for myself, inhaling deeply. My mind was mush from all that had happened. When I was ready, I looked at myself in the mirror. My hair was a mess, going every which way, and my eyes were red from crying. I swallowed hard and turned my back to the mirror, then looked over my shoulder. I winced and touched my ass softly. My butt looked like two tomatoes, the skin red and swollen. There were some spots where it was darker. I assumed that was where the paddle had landed. I couldn't deny that I was fascinated by what had happened. I couldn't explain it, but somehow the spanking made me feel closer to Gabriel.

Deciding I was too exhausted to think on it more, I brushed my teeth and tried to make myself look decent for him. When I was done, I reluctantly stepped out. He was in his massive closet, fiddling with something. When he saw me, he smiled, then disappeared into the bathroom. I sighed, looking around the room. I listened to him move around, turn the water on and off, the toilet flush.

When he exited, he pulled his tank over his head. "Get into bed."

"Yes, sir," I said, and slipped in, wincing as the sheets slid across my sore butt. I shifted my weight onto my side, then proceeded to watch Gabriel as he removed his pants. With the lights fully on, I gaped at the sight of all that manly perfection. He was absolutely gorgeous. He discarded his clothes into the hamper, then moved back into the closet.

When he finally came to join me in bed, I didn't react much, which was strange. I thought I should be nervous, not just of the situation, but because the last time I'd been here, panic had followed. He sat down, then turned off the lamp, but the light from the closet spilled into the room, bathing the furniture in a soft glow.

Gabriel rolled over toward me and pulled the sheets over us. With the light, I could see his face, his lips quirked up into a soft smile. "This okay?"

"Yes, sir. Thank you, sir," I croaked. "Thank you for… making sure…."

He wrapped an arm around my back and pulled me close. "While in bed, you are allowed to touch me. And did I not tell you that a master takes care of his slave?"

I managed a faint smile. "Yes, sir."

When I didn't move, he took my arm and set it against his side so that I could feel the strong muscles of his back. I fell into him, daring to get closer, and closed my eyes, his scent filling me.

"Remember what I said before." He spoke softly. "Should I require something in the middle of the night, it will be your responsibility to fulfill it."

"Yes, sir," I confirmed.

"Good boy," he whispered.

I was surprised as weariness hit me like a truck, and I fell asleep to his thumb stroking my back.

 Eight

"JOEY."

I lolled my head. I knew that voice. It took me a moment to realize it was Gabriel. When I peeled my eyes open, he was sitting up in his big bed, looking down on me. He was freshly groomed and dressed comfortably in a form-fitting T-shirt and jeans. I furrowed my brows. I'd never seen him look so relaxed before.

"Good morning, slave," he teased, then got up. "It's late and time for you to get up. Go take a shower and prepare yourself for me. Then meet me in my office. You have thirty minutes."

"Yes, sir," I mumbled, shielding my eyes from the bright sunlight streaming in through the balcony. The double doors were wide open, the sound of birds singing coming in. The air was warm, comfortable. The nice weather heightened my good mood.

I took a few minutes to relax, feeling light and hopeful, but I didn't want to make him wait so I dragged my feet into the bathroom. I immediately inspected my behind. It was still blushing, though maybe not quite as much as it had been last night, but the welts were more clearly defined. I touched my butt gingerly—it was still hot.

I quickly relieved myself, then stepped into the shower, purposely running cool water over my backside. Yeah, that felt nice. I knew it was going to be irritating me all day. I didn't bother washing my hair, as I already had the day before, but made sure to scrub my body well, purposely avoiding my butt. I ran my hands all over but didn't feel any stubble, the skin smooth and slick.

I turned off the water and stepped out, wrapping a giant black towel around my shoulders. I dried myself thoroughly, then started finger combing my hair when I realized my backpack was sitting in a corner. Gabriel must have brought it in. I had taken some personal care items with me, so I dug in and pulled out a comb, deodorant, a razor, and shaving cream. I did the best I could with what I had, then stepped out into the bedroom. When I was in front of Gabriel's office, I took several deep breaths. When I was ready, I knocked.

"Come in," he said.

I pushed my way in and closed the door behind me. Gabriel was at his desk, lazing against the chair, apparently waiting for me, looking optimistic. My eyes fell to the crop on his desk. He had said we would resume training today, and I was looking forward to it, though I hoped he spared my spanked ass a little.

I presented myself in the middle of the room, trying to hide my wince as my legs pressed against my ass. I straightened my spine and waited for him.

"How are you feeling?" he inquired.

"Okay, sir," I said. "A little sore, but… excited."

"On your feet," he commanded, and I obeyed, happy to be off my behind.

He came around to join me, his eyes tracking me with heat. He must have liked what he saw, because he grinned like a wolf. Then his hands were on me, skimming my chest, gliding down my belly. When he gripped my cock, I gasped.

"Smooth. Nice," he observed. "Lean over my desk."

"Yes, sir," I said and did as ordered.

His hands were cool on my ass, heavy but gentle, and I closed my eyes. His fingers ran down my taint to my ball sac, and when he dragged them back up my crack, I moaned from the sensation.

117

"Was I not clear?" he asked, his tone even. "Did I not tell you that the next time you came to me, you would be bare here?"

I blushed, a little embarrassed. I stumbled for an excuse. "I didn't know how…. I'm sorry, sir."

"You could have asked me," he said, taking his hands away. "Twenty points."

I hung my head low. "Yes, sir."

He stepped away, and I craned my neck to the side. I watched as he wrote in my book. I was so close to another hundred that I was sure I was going to be punished again before the weekend was out. I just hoped it wasn't another spanking. At this rate I wouldn't be able to sit down.

When he was done recording my indiscretion, he moved over toward the couch, retrieved the bottle of oil, and squirted some into his hands. He returned to me, then spread the oil all over my ass. I sighed, the soothing aloe doing wonders for my sore bum.

"Is there anything you would like to talk about, Joey?" he asked, his hands still on my ass. "I want you to communicate to me your feelings, whether it be concern or curiosity."

"I feel…." I bit my lip in indecision. "I don't know, strangely content. I'm still somewhat shaken up about what happened, but at the same time I feel hopeful… if that makes any sense?"

"That's good," he said. "I will remind you again that the past is behind us. Are you ready to continue your training, Joey?"

I moaned softly. "Yes, sir. I really am."

"Good boy," he said, and I knew he was smiling. "Come with me."

"Yes, sir," I confirmed, and followed him down the stairs and into the kitchen.

"Do you like Wheaties?" he inquired.

"Ah… yes, actually… sir." I had been caught off guard by the question, but at the mention of food, my stomach rumbled. I'd probably lost a pound or two during the week. I just hadn't been able to eat, and I was skinny enough as it was.

"Retrieve two bowls and two spoons," Gabriel said.

"Yes, sir." I found the bowls and gathered some silverware, then came to join Gabriel by the counter.

He poured some cereal into the bowls, popping a Wheatie into his mouth. "Hope you don't mind skim milk."

"No, sir."

"Should you decide to sign a contract with me, I will acquire food that you like. As a diabetic, there is a lot that I can't eat, so things like regular sugar or whole milk don't exist in this house," he explained, pouring the milk into the bowls.

"Thank you, sir," I said, truly meaning it.

He took his bowl and sat down.

"Do you need anything else, sir?" I inquired.

"No, come sit down."

I obeyed, setting my cereal on the table. I sat down, not paying attention, and groaned. I cursed to myself and tried to get as comfortable as possible in my condition. It wasn't the best position, but it would have to do. We ate in silence, Gabriel glancing at the newspaper folded on the table. As soon as I had taken my first bite, my hunger returned full force, and when I was done, I was still hungry. I glanced longingly at the cereal box.

"If you are still hungry, feel free to get some more," Gabriel said, his eyes on the newspaper. It was amazing the way he noticed things.

"Thank you, sir," I said, and loaded my bowl with delicious wheat flakes.

"Before you sit down, put this in the sink," he said, holding out his bowl.

I came and took it from him, then set it in the sink. As I ate my second helping, he leaned back in his chair and unfolded the paper. He slipped his glasses on, and I watched, transfixed, as his brows lowered and his lip rose in a silent snarl. I guessed he didn't like what he was reading.

I returned my attention to my food and devoured it, sipping the milk from the bowl quietly. When I was done, I got up, thankful to be off my sore ass. I set the bowl in the sink and put everything away, making sure the cereal box was sealed. I knew Gabriel didn't like stale cereal any more than I did. I heard the paper crinkle as if it was being thrown down, and a colorful curse followed. I couldn't help but to smile to myself. Gabriel was sexy when he was angry, at least when he wasn't angry with me.

He glanced at his watch before saying, "I have some tasks for you. Are you paying attention?"

"Yes, sir." I turned to give him my full attention.

"In the bathroom and bedroom you will find a hamper. Collect all the clothes—you can use the basket found next to the dryer. You know where the laundry room is. If you wish to wash your clothes, add them to the pile. On the shelf just above the washing machine are two bottles. You will use the one on the left. Before you dump everything in, separate my underwear from the pile. You will wash those by hand using the bottle on the right. Put everything into the dryer, and use three dryer sheets. Once that is done, if you'll look in the cabinet over the shelf to the left side, you will find a bottle of leather conditioner and a chamois cloth. You are to go up to my office and clean your tears from my couch. While you're there, return the paddle to the room directly across from my office on the left wall in between the cat-o'-nine-tails and the cane. Also, my bed needs to be remade. I'm giving you two hours to complete your assignment, so manage your time wisely. Pay attention to where things are. I expect you to put everything back as you've found them."

"Yes, sir," I said, and bolted for the stairs.

"Walk, don't run," he hissed.

I skidded to a slower pace. "Yes, sir. Sorry, sir."

I found the hamper basket in the bathroom full of towels and the one in his room filled to the top with his clothes. As I gathered them, I realized I had forgotten the laundry basket downstairs. I decided to improvise, stuffing everything into the hamper, then lugging it down the stairs. Gabriel was still at the table, reading, when I made for the laundry room. I threw everything into the washer, plucking his boxers from the pile and setting them in the sink. I selected the bottle on the left and poured a little in, then tightened the cap so he couldn't find fault. After I turned the washer on, I filled the sink up halfway with hot water, then began the arduous task of scrubbing his underwear with the soap from the bottle on the right. It was weird to me, but whatever, it was what Gabriel had commanded I do.

By the time I had gotten through the three pairs, the clothes in the washer were done, so I stuck everything into the dryer and threw some fabric sheets in. I located the leather conditioner and cloth and brought the hamper back upstairs with me. While I was in his bedroom, I made the bed, carefully pushing out any wrinkles. When I entered his office, my eyes immediately settled on the wooden paddle lying on the table. I unconsciously touched my behind. I swore I could still feel it.

Shivering, I decided to put it away first. It was strange; it felt so much lighter in my palm. When it had fallen against my ass, it had felt more like a two-by-four. I traced the little holes with my finger—I knew what they were for. During my Internet adventures, I had learned that the holes allowed for airflow, creating a swifter swing. I hoped I never gave Gabriel another opportunity to use it against me again, although the way he spoke about his cane.... I didn't think anything could be worse than what I had endured last night.

I stepped into the room opposite his office and flipped the light switch then... gaped. I was sure I was going to need surgery to reattach my jaw. There were several black dressers outlining the walls, but what really caught my attention were the tools hanging on hooks: whips, paddles, floggers, canes....

I couldn't breathe as I neared an empty hook flanked by a leather whip with trails of braided leather and a mean-looking bamboo cane. My hands shook as I hung the wooden paddle between its friends. The tools scared me, and yet... I wanted to feel each one, just to *know*....

I didn't understand the desire, and it startled me, so I quickly abandoned the room, closing the door behind me. I had to take several deep breaths to steady myself. When I was ready, I returned to Gabriel's office and thoroughly cleaned the leather. I'd never cared for leather before, but the directions on the back of the bottle were fairly straightforward. I hoped Gabriel approved of my efforts.

When I came back downstairs, Gabriel was in the living room on the couch, his head back as if he were sleeping. I was quiet as I returned the cleaning supplies to the cabinet. The dryer had stopped, so I pulled everything out and dumped it into the basket. I double-checked my work, sure I had done everything according to his directions.

I bit my lip as I entered the living room. He was indeed sleeping, his eyes closed, his breath even. I wasn't sure what to do but decided not to disturb him. I presented myself next to the couch, careful to put as little weight on my legs as possible. As the minutes passed, I slumped and adjusted my position several times. I guessed it would take me a while to get used to sitting in this position. Then again, my sore ass wasn't exactly helping.

A soft chime went off, and Gabriel came awake. He squinted at his watch, then silenced it. When he glanced at me, I perfected my position.

"You finish your chores?" he asked, ruffling his hair.

"Yes, sir."

He got up and stretched, that shirt hugging his body wonderfully. He circled around me, and I knew he was looking for any inconsistencies in my posture. Apparently pleased, he headed for the laundry room. I mentally checked my work, hoping I'd done everything as he'd asked.

"Joey, come here," he called.

I sighed and got to my feet. When I entered the room, he was going through the basket of clothes. "Yes, sir?"

He held up a pair of white socks that had turned a blotchy gray. I flushed, looking down.

He chuckled. "What's wrong?"

"Ah... sorry, sir?"

"Did I tell you to separate the whites?" he inquired.

"No, sir." I frowned.

"Then why are you apologizing? You followed my directions." He tossed them in the garbage. "The fault was mine. I didn't realize I had anything white in the hamper. Joey, I will never blame you for something that is out of your control or shift my mistake onto you. Do you understand?"

I couldn't help but beam at him. "Yes, sir. Thank you, sir."

He ruffled my hair, the caress making me soar inside.

He chuckled. "I've only counted two dryer sheets. Did I not say three?"

"Ah, yes, sir, you did. I thought I had...."

"Did you count them?" he asked, turning his attention to me. His face was light, his body loose.

I sighed, wanting to bonk myself in the head. "No, sir."

He nodded. "Come."

I followed Gabriel up the stairs and into his office. He checked the couch, running his palm over the leather, then said, "Present yourself."

"Yes, sir," I confirmed and assumed the proper position.

He left the room, and I listened as doors were opened and closed, his footfalls making the floor creak. I was still mad at myself for messing up on the dryer sheets, but he seemed happy with my efforts. He returned, snatching my book and pen from the table, then sat on his desk.

His eyes fell on me. "Good job, Joey. With exception to the incorrect number of dryer sheets used, you did everything as I asked. I'm assigning you five points for missing that detail."

I was filled with pride and hope and all sorts of good stuff as he wrote in my book, even though I'd earned more points.

When he was done, he snapped it shut and asked, "Do you know why I scrutinized the details?"

"Ah...." I bit my lip. "No, sir."

"Of course, you will be required to carry out chores, but the point I am trying to make is that you must pay careful attention to my orders. It lets me know that you are paying attention to me, that your ultimate goal is to please me. If I do not have your full attention, then that means you have other priorities than serving me. Do you understand what I am telling you?"

"Yes, sir. I do." I nodded.

"Good boy. I'm proud of your efforts." He smiled. "Now, get dressed. We are going out."

"Yes, sir," I barked enthusiastically, beyond elated that he was happy with me.

GABRIEL PARKED the Camaro in the rear lot, and we got out. I was surprised when he threw an arm around my shoulders, pulling me close as we walked into the building. It felt so very nice, as if I had been claimed by this wonderful man. I knew that an *It* wouldn't receive such touches or be praised for his hard work. I was so very glad that Gabriel held a certain respect for me.

When we entered, I noticed that it was some sort of spa, the lights low, the air thick with the scent of water and flowers. It was warm too, way hotter than the sixty-degree spring air outside.

"Mason-San, so nice to see you again," an Asian woman said with a thick accent, bowing her head slightly.

"Thank you. I called this morning and set an appointment with Min," he said, his arm slipping from my shoulders. I missed the weight and the warmth.

"*Hai*, right this way." She smiled.

I followed behind Gabriel as the woman led us into a locker room of sorts, then left us to our own devices. Gabriel started stripping, drawing his shirt over his head.

"Remove your clothes, Joey," he ordered.

"Y-yes, sir," I said and stripped.

He took my clothes and shoes from me and stuck them into a locker, securing the lock then handing me a towel. I watched as he wrapped the towel around his waist, and I followed his example, the scratchy fabric not entirely pleasant against my butt. When we exited the locker room, there was another tiny woman of Asian descent waiting for us.

"I'm ready for you, Mr. Mason." She grinned, her expression hiding something.

"Lead on, ma'am." He tipped his head.

Min took us around the corner and into a private room, the air clearer. There was some sort of table in the center with half of it raised like a hospital bed.

"Joey is new to this, so I'm going to show him how it's done," Gabriel said to her, whipping his towel off.

She tipped her head and held her hand out toward the table.

I watched in shock as he got up on the table, then leaned over the raised end. Min turned her attention to the side, where a pot of some sort was cooking, the steam curling into the air. Normally, Gabriel's stark-naked form would have grabbed my attention, but as Min snapped on a pair of gloves and poured some sort of concoction into a bowl, I gaped. Oh my God.... Was he really?

Gabriel spread his cheeks for her, and she applied what I was pretty sure was wax up and down his crack.

"Joey, you're not going to pass out on me, are you?" Gabriel teased.

"What?"

Gabriel looked at Min behind him. "Amateur."

She giggled. When she was satisfied with her job, she retrieved some sort of paper and pressed it over the wax. They made small talk as I stood there with my jaw on the floor, Gabriel's tone light, as if they did this on a regular basis.

Min returned to his ass, and I swallowed hard. Gabriel had bumped his head against the table, apparently preparing himself. When she yanked the paper away, I winced, but Gabriel simply took a deep breath and laughed. Then he flipped over and spread his legs. I watched in shock as she spread wax over his balls and the creases in between his legs. When she ripped the paper off, I looked away, but Gabriel didn't make a sound of discomfort.

He laughed and slipped off the table, snatched a cloth from a dispenser on the wall, and dried himself. I stared at him wide-eyed as he pulled me against his body. He gripped my arm and pressed my palm to his ass. I didn't hesitate, spanning his crack, the skin smooth. I wasn't sure when I would have the opportunity to touch him like this again, so I exploited it.

"Feels good, huh?" He grinned.

"Yes… sir." I breathed out, unable to keep the smile from my lips.

My towel was pulled away from my hips. "Your turn."

My smile fell as I looked at the table. Min was waiting for me, her hands in front of her waist, a pleasant smile on her lips. Reluctantly, I approached the table and clumsily climbed on.

Min giggled. "Looks like someone has been a naughty boy."

I blushed and was sure my cheeks matched the color of my ass. Gabriel came to stand in front of me, his eyes light with mischief, his lips quirked. "Spread your cheeks as if you are offering for me."

I swallowed hard and did as told, feeling exposed. I still wasn't completely comfortable naked in front of Gabriel, but another person? Yeah…. Still his words penetrated me, and I parted my ass for *him*, because it was what he desired. If he wanted me hairless and smooth there, then I'd do it because I wanted to please him. He held me with his eyes as the hot wax was applied. It didn't burn, but the heat made me sweat. I felt the paper pressed against me and then… nothing.

"The great thing is that if you keep doing this, the hair will get thinner, and after a while, you'll have to do it less and less," Gabriel explained, keeping my attention. "It will sting at first, but you get used to it."

"You do this a lot?" I asked, curious.

"Once a month now," he said, resting his head on his hand. After a few minutes, he said, "Take a deep breath."

I did, and—my skin was ripped from my body. At least it felt like it. I bumped my head against the edge of the table and barked, "Fuckity fuck fuck!"

I heard Gabriel laugh darkly. "It will pass. Just breathe."

The instant fire along my crack was almost as bad as that wooden paddle falling against my spanked ass, but Gabriel was right—it started to subside, the sting easing.

"Will there be anything else that may require my services, or should I inform my colleagues to prepare for you?" I heard Min ask.

"No, that's it. Thanks, Min," he said.

I heard the snapping of gloves, then the click of the door and managed to slide off the table. Gabriel handed me a cloth, and I dried myself, then tossed the cloth into a waste bin. Gabriel came forth with a small bottle and squeezed some lotion into his hands. He ran it up and down my crack. It felt so nice… his slick fingers slipping and sliding in such an intimate place. I actually moaned.

When he was done, he grabbed my hand and squirted some lotion in my palm, then pushed my hand into the crack of his ass. I didn't hesitate, spreading it up and down, purposely drawing it out. I was just so glad being allowed to touch him freely that I smiled so hard my cheeks hurt.

He chuckled. "I'm going to have a lot of fun with you when we get home."

I closed my eyes and sighed at his words. I couldn't wait. I felt the towel wrap around my waist, and Gabriel secured it, his fingers grazing my stomach. That touch lit me up, my cock hardening just a little.

"Come," he said.

At first I thought he was giving me permission to orgasm, but as he walked out the door, I mentally bonked myself on the forehead.... My thoughts were in the gutter. I followed behind, and he led us into a room where two women waited. I could smell incense burning somewhere, and soft oriental music played overhead. There were two tables in the center of the room with something that looked like a padded toilet seat at the top end. Gabriel strutted over to one and hopped on, lying on his belly. He rested his head against the U-shaped cushion.

I took my own table, getting comfortable, glad that the towel was still wrapped around my hips. I didn't want anyone else to see my flushed butt. It was weird at first, but I got comfortable on the table, my face pushing through the cushion. I heard the women move around and then there was the scent of oil and... hands touched me, spreading oil all over my back.

I sighed and relaxed. The woman had magic hands. She kneaded me well, working out the tightness in my back, her fingers smoothing out little knots. I groaned in pleasure.

"How you doing over there, Joey?" Gabriel asked, muffled.

"Very good, sir... very... yeah," I moaned, and heard him chuckle.

Just when I thought it was over, I felt her hands start to work my thighs, and I entered an all-new high, smiling like an idiot. I'd never had a massage before, other than a light back rub from Hanny when I was a kid. But this was ridiculous. I wasn't sure how much time had passed, and by the time she got to my calves, I had entered a trance, my mind zoning out. Before I knew it, the massage was over and we were alone. It had been so worth the pain and embarrassment of getting my ass waxed.

"Joey?" Gabriel called.

I craned my neck to look at him, a goofy smile on my face. "Huh?"

He grinned, and I took a moment to appreciate how beautiful he was when he smiled. "Good, huh?"

"Oh, yessss, sir… thank you."

He held out his hand, and I took it. When I got on my feet, I realized I had an erection the size of a cucumber. I laughed and noticed Gabriel had one too.

"It happens." He shrugged. "Let's get going."

"Yes, sir," I mumbled, feeling better than I had in a very long time.

Nine

AFTER THE trip to the spa, Gabriel took me to a deli. I'd never before imagined I would use the words gourmet and sandwich in the same sentence. It was ridiculously delicious. As he had done at Olympus, whatever we didn't finish went into a container and was handed over to some homeless people. By the time we got back to his house, it was almost five.

"Did you enjoy yourself, Joey?" he asked as we took our shoes off.

"Yes, sir, very much. Thank you." I nodded, feeling light.

"When I'm not swamped with work, I enjoy going out. Should you decide to enter into a contract with me, you can expect more days like this. Contrary to what you might think, you are not a prisoner here. Should you want to do something like see a movie, simply make a request, and I will consider it."

I let out a breath. "Thank you, sir."

"Come with me. I want to explain something to you," he said.

I followed Gabriel upstairs to the bathroom. He surprised me by pulling me close, his hands cupping my ass gently. He chuckled, popping the button on my jeans. "We need to get these off of you."

I smiled. "I couldn't agree more, sir."

I let him undress me, pulling my shirt over my head and pushing my pants down so that they pooled around my ankles. Then he was pressing his lips against my shoulder. I wanted to touch him so bad, feel his skin under my palms, but I managed to control my hands. I felt fingers dip into my crack, stroking, exploring.

"Yeah... so much fun," he whispered, then broke away. "Look in the cabinet behind you on the bottom shelf to the very left."

I did as told and found some boxes stacked against one another. On the front was a picture of a bottle and long nozzle, and... *oh*. I blushed fiercely.

"I demand that you be prepared for me, both outside and inside. When and if you enter into my service, this will become a common occurrence," he explained. I was so embarrassed, I couldn't look at him. "Generally, I will let you know when I want to fuck you, and it will be your responsibility to see that you are ready for me. Joey, eyes here."

I tried really hard to look at him, I really did, but I could only get to his jaw.

"Does this scare you, Joey?" he asked, his tone thick with curiosity.

"Ah...." I ran my fingers through my hair. "It's... embarrassing."

"Why?" He frowned. "Enemas have been proven to provide many health benefits. Regardless, it is nonnegotiable. I will give you the privacy you want, but you have thirty minutes to present yourself to me in my office, clean and ready. Do you understand?"

I gaped but managed a faint "Yes, sir."

When the bathroom door closed, I reluctantly dragged my eyes to the boxes. I was grateful he didn't want me to do it in front of him. I wasn't sure I could, even if I wanted to. His explanation made total sense, but it was still weird to me. Back in high school, kids had made jokes about enemas, and the butt rinse had generally been regarded as something done by "old people." I sighed and grabbed a box. If I did this, then Gabriel might fuck me tonight. That was all the encouragement I needed.

I extracted the bottle from the box, then removed the cellophane wrapping and dumped it into the garbage. I proceeded to stare at the bottle the way I had when I'd seen a condom for the first time. I'd had no idea what to do with it and had settled for turning it into a water balloon. Biting my lip, I recovered the box from the trash and read the directions. Okay, so it was straightforward enough.

I managed to administer it easily, but geez, it felt weird. I leaned over the counter and concentrated on holding it for the five minutes the box had recommended. I counted the seconds in my head, the counter cool against me. When time was up, I took my seat on the throne and was thankful to get it out of me.

I knew I was never going to forget this—if only because of the weirdness factor. When I was done, I tidied up a bit, making sure everything was clean and in its place. I folded my clothes and set them on a shelf. I had quickly learned that Gabriel was a bit of a neat freak, and I didn't want him to find anything out of order.

I knocked on his office door and heard him grant me permission.

Gabriel was at his desk, leaning back against his chair. He was shirtless, and his hand was working on something below the desk. I presented myself in the middle of the room as required.

He smirked. "I didn't scar you for life, did I?"

I couldn't help but smile shyly. "No, sir. It was just a little weird. I've never had one before."

"Understandable," he said. "Come here."

I didn't hesitate, getting to my feet and coming around to join him. I swallowed hard. He wasn't shirtless, he was *naked*, his cock engorged and lying against his belly as if waiting for me. He scooted forward and gripped my hips, then spun me around. I let him guide me, pressing my torso against the desk so that he had access to my ass. His hands were gentle as he squeezed my cheeks. I was still sore, but his hands felt nice. My jaw fell open in a silent gasp as he pressed a kiss against one of the welts.

"You're no longer blushing like a strawberry." He chuckled.

I had meant to respond, but as his tongue lapped at my skin, I hissed. Gabriel kissed every inch of my spanked bottom, paying special attention to where the paddle had branded me. I actually relaxed against the cool desk, his ministrations comforting.

"Spread your legs," he commanded.

I obeyed, and when I felt a single finger run down my crack, I whimpered.

"So smooth," he purred. "Should you wish to wax the rest of your body instead of shave, I will temporarily suspend the requirement for you to be clean shaven. The hair needs to be a certain length before it can be plucked."

"Thank you, sir," I muttered.

His finger skimmed back up, grazing my asshole. Then he was cupping my nut sac, his palm warm.

"Please!" I gasped when he pushed at my hole with his thumb. "Sir...."

Gabriel chuckled, the sound a dark curl. "You want me to fill this little hole of yours?"

"Please, sir," I begged.

"Hm...," he purred. "I have something for you. Turn around."

I managed to obey, my body weak. My cock was hard, jutting out from my hips, begging for release, but I knew I would be lucky if he allowed me to come tonight. Gabriel maneuvered me onto his desk, spreading my legs. He reached into his drawer and produced another dildo, this one the perfect likeness of a cock. It looked a little bigger than the stacked ball plug, but not as large as Gabriel was.

"Yeah, this will look wonderful in you," he said, his eyes running along the dong's length.

When his eyes snapped to me, I bit my lip. I watched in astonishment as he ran the tip of the dildo along my thigh toward my crotch. When it hit my asshole, I threw my head back and moaned softly. It teased me, the cool, smooth rubber hardly touching my skin, and then it was gone, just like that. When I craned my head to see what was happening, I found Gabriel looking at me like a wolf looks at a steak.

"Tell me how bad you want it," he commanded, his voice hoarse.

I begged for him, begged him to slide it into me, to fuck me with it. His smile grew with every word, and I was surprised by the desperation in my voice. But I needed something, anything he was willing to give me. He had seemed pleased with me all day, and I prayed he would reward me for services well rendered.

"You want it? Then get it nice and slick," he growled, pressing the dong to my lips.

I didn't hesitate. I parted my lips and took it into my mouth. It didn't taste all that pleasant, but I didn't care. I had become a ravenous beast needing one thing. I sucked on the fake cock, bobbing my head back and forth, trying to slick it so it would slide into me easily. Gabriel seemed pleased with my efforts, pushing the dong in and out of my mouth.

He took it away from me and pressed it against my hole, and I arched into it, needing to feel it stretch me. I felt my muscles part, accepting the intrusion, the rubber feeling so cool against my hot asshole. "Please, sir...."

Gabriel tried to give me a little more, but my saliva wasn't enough to ensure a smooth trip, so to speak. I whimpered like a lonely little puppy.

"Aw...," Gabriel cooed. "Poor slave."

He produced a tube of lube and squirted some on top of the dong. It seemed like forever as he tossed the tube away and returned the dildo to my ass. As soon as I felt the cool moisture, I pressed into the dong. The head slipped into me, and I moaned.

"Easy, boy," Gabriel growled softly. "I know you want it, but you're only going to get what I choose to give you."

"Yes, sir. Sorry, sir," I croaked, trying to keep myself from thrusting against the toy.

Gabriel tortured me, pushing the dong into me just a little. I instantly noticed it was a little bigger than the stacked balls, but it felt good, and when he gave me more, I gasped. He was careful not to hurt me, the new feeling bordering on discomfort, but that was part of the thrill. I groaned as he slowly slid it into me, filling and stretching me until it could go no farther.

"Good boy," he whispered and pressed a hand against my chest. "Lay back against the desk."

I obeyed, pressing my back to the cool wood. Gabriel pulled me toward him, my butt off the desk, and I rested my head on the hard surface. He balanced me with my legs over his shoulders, until I felt the supple leather of his office chair touch my toes. As the dildo was languorously withdrawn from me, I gripped the edge of the desk for support.

Gabriel pushed it back into me as slowly as he had taken it away, and my mouth opened in shocked pleasure. All discomfort had melted away, and I was left with nothing but pure pleasure. My cock was red and swollen in the air, my fingers gripping into the desk. I knew Gabriel was going to destroy me with pleasure—and it was going to be awesome.

I moaned softly as he slowly fucked me with the dildo. I didn't need to see his face to know he was grinning at me like a demon, all sly intention. I don't know how long he tortured me, but it felt like years, and just when I thought I'd go mad from the slow burn, he started fucking me in quick, short strokes. I bowed my spine and cried out shamelessly. It felt so good I could hardly stand it.

Gabriel growled something fierce, and the dong was pulled out of me. I didn't get a chance to beg for more because he flipped me back onto my stomach and pressed my body against the desk. I felt him come closer, felt the heat of his body, and then his cock was brushing up against my ass—hard and silky-smooth skin.

"Please, sir, fuck me! I need to feel you," I begged. "Please... I need your cock in me."

He planted a kiss on my shoulder. "Oh, I want to so bad, Joey. But I won't unless you commit yourself to me." He dug his fingers into my hair and pulled my head back, speaking against my ear. "But do not think I am trying to manipulate you into signing a contract with me. Do you understand? I may be a crafty bastard, but I want your first to be… special. Even if it's not with me."

I gaped, astounded by this man. It was a wonder how he could be so sweet and harsh at the same time.

He chuckled. "At least I got to claim your first spanking."

He landed a heavy hand on my sore bum, and I gasped, the sting lighting me up. I heard him laugh, and then my ass cheeks were spread and his hot length thrust up and down my crack.

"Get up on the desk a little more," he said hoarsely.

I scooted forward so that my chest was off the desk. I used my hands to hold on as Gabriel thrust against my crack, stroking himself between my ass cheeks. His breathing picked up, his hands gripping onto my shoulders for leverage. An idea popped into my head. I squeezed my ass cheeks, and he groaned.

"Oh, fuck… that's it, slave," he growled. "Tighten that ass."

I couldn't help but beam as he rubbed against me, the force of his thrusts slowly pushing me off the desk. And then he was roaring like a vicious animal, hot cum pouring onto my back. It took him several minutes to come down, his hands tight on my shoulders, his hips flush against my behind.

"I should punish you for making me lose control," he said, slipping away.

He cracked my ass a good one, and I barked a curse as the sting fired through me, but then he was stroking my ass gently, his palms soothing over the hurt. I felt his lips touch me where he had slapped me, and I sighed, the kiss tender.

"Thank you, sir," I muttered.

He chuckled softly. "Why are you thanking me, slave?"

"For letting me pleasure you, sir."

He made a sound of satisfaction, then got up. His tight ass flashed in front of me before he stepped out of the room. I sighed as I lay on the desk. Even though I was monstrously aroused and was sure I wasn't going to be coming anytime soon, I was… happy.

He returned quickly, wiping his crotch with a washcloth. He cleaned the mess from my back, and I heard him settle into his chair with a huge sigh of contentment.

"Nice view back here," he teased.

I grinned. "I'm glad, sir."

After a few moments, he gathered me in his arms and pressed me against his body, my ass on his leg. My head fell back against his shoulder, and I sighed.

"Thank you, sir," I murmured.

He held me like this for a short while, his minty breath filling my nose, the warmth of his body keeping me comfortable. His hand, which had been on my stomach, slowly slid down to grip my aching cock. It had remained hard, my balls tense. I wanted to beg that he let me come, but honestly, I liked that he controlled my orgasms. It wasn't something that I could explain; it just was.

Gabriel chuckled as he plucked a rubber band from his drawer. He whispered into my ear, "I know you like these things. Have you ever put some on your cock, Joey?"

I moaned softly and nodded. "Sometimes."

"Did you like it?"

"Yes, sir."

He gave me the rubber band, and I took it.

"Do it," he commanded.

I obeyed, slipping my cock through the band, then twisting it so I could secure the band just behind my glans. I hissed as it constricted my cock. Gabriel handed me another, and another, until my dick was nearly covered by colored bands of rubber.

"Not too tight, is it?" Gabriel asked.

"No... sir...," I whispered. It was perfect, the tightness just enough, the texture strange, yet welcomed.

Gabriel chuckled and batted my dick, and I arched my back. He pushed me gently, and I got up.

"Follow," he said simply, and we went downstairs.

Gabriel took a seat on the couch, and I presented myself in the normal spot, awaiting further instruction. He turned the television on and flipped to CNN, then leaned back and propped his feet up on an ottoman. I could do nothing but sit there, my cock hard and aching. I wanted to join him, feel his body against mine. My attention stayed on him. Every now and then, his lip rose in a silent snarl, apparently agitated with the news report. I could feel my muscles tensing, waiting for the moment when—

He patted the seat, and that was all I needed. I scrambled to my feet and came to sit next to him, his arm going around my shoulders and pulling me against his chest. He gave me permission to touch him, and I wrapped an arm around his waist.

"Thank you, sir," I said softly and fell into him.

I closed my eyes, intent on enjoying the moment. His thumb stroked my shoulder, his chest slowly rising and falling. He whispered curses at the television, made rogue comments on how people were idiots. Slowly, his hand drifted down to my belly, then to my cock. I gasped softly as he played with me, removing one rubber band at a time. I was so aroused that I was leaking, but he didn't seem to care.

I wasn't sure how much time had passed, his hands driving me insane, but when the last rubber band popped off, I breathed a sigh of relief. My cock was swollen and red and... I really needed to come. Gabriel kept me hard for a long time, his fingers playing with my glans, his hand stroking me slowly until I was moaning softly against his shirt. I heard him curse and kill the television, but my mind was mush from arousal. I could think of nothing else, and I prayed that he'd be merciful and let me come.

"It's late," he said. "Let's head upstairs."

138

"Yes, sir," I mumbled. Oh God, how was I ever going to sleep tonight?

When we came into his room, he pushed me onto the bed. His smile was mischievous, his eyes aglow in the low light of the room.

"Please, sir," I heard myself whimper.

"Hm, you have been a good boy today," he purred. "I think you should be rewarded."

My mouth fell open in a silent gasp. I wanted to beg that he let me come, but I couldn't find my voice. Just as well, though, because he came to kneel before me and pushed my legs apart. Then his lips were on my stomach, kissing, nipping, his tongue searing me. Without warning, he pushed me against the bed roughly, and I moaned as his tongue licked a path up the side of my ball sac.

I dug my fingers into the sheets—I knew one touch was going to send me into orgasm. Gabriel was merciless, running his hot tongue up and down my smooth skin, and when he dragged the very tip of his tongue up my shaft, I started begging. He didn't grant me release, not yet, his wicked lips and tongue working in sync to drive me mad.

Only when I was a mess did he give me permission to come. My body quaked, my balls tightened, the orgasm destroying me. I could hardly think as pleasure assaulted me, Gabriel working between my legs. He took all I had to offer until the stimulation became painful.

He chuckled, giving my cock a final, playful swat. I gasped at the strange pleasure-pain and collapsed on the bed. I watched in a daze as he retrieved something from his dresser drawer. It was a watch of sorts.

"It will be your duty to wake before me and prepare yourself as well as breakfast," he said, then came next to me and slipped the watch onto my wrist. "The watch will vibrate when it goes off, but I'm going to set it so that it also chimes. I recommend using both so that your brain learns to associate the vibration with the ring."

"Yes, sir," I said hoarsely as he secured it to my wrist.

He cupped my chin in his hand and made me look at him. "Pay attention. When you wake in the morning, you will have an hour to prepare yourself and make breakfast. On the second shelf to the left, you will find a carton of Egg Beaters. Cook two servings' worth in a pan. Then you will make me two slices of toast—no butter or jelly. Breakfast usually only takes about ten minutes to make, but as soon as you get downstairs, you should start the coffeepot. By the time I come into the kitchen, my coffee should be ready and hot, my breakfast prepared. Any questions?"

I thought for a moment. "No, sir."

"Good. If I find anything to my dissatisfaction, points will be given," he warned.

"Yes, sir," I acknowledged.

Gabriel went into his closet and turned the light on, then joined me in bed. He scooped me up, cuddling me close, our bodies entwining. The warmth of his presence and the smoothness of his skin helped me to relax. I was surprised at how safe I felt in this man's arms. Just like before, I fell asleep to his fingers stroking me gently.

Ten

SOMETHING HIT me on my ass, and I jerked awake, the sting startling me. It was Gabriel, and… I realized the watch he had given me was going off. I cursed and scrambled to kill it. When I got it to turn off, I looked at the man next to me. His eyes were hooded from sleep, his hair a sexy mess.

"Sorry, sir."

He made a sound of acknowledgment and turned on his other side, then went back to sleep.

I narrowed my eyes on the watch, everything still hazy. It was eight fifteen, which meant I had forty-five minutes to get myself ready and make him breakfast. I was already fifteen minutes behind, so I rushed through a shower, washing my body and hair. I couldn't help but glance at the box of enemas lined up neatly in the closet. I dried myself as I ran down the stairs.

I quickly discarded the towel in the laundry room, then gathered the ingredients from the fridge. I started the coffee and retrieved a flat pan to cook the Egg Beaters in. The toast was easy, and as the slices of bread popped up, I heard Gabriel walking around upstairs. He came down about fifteen minutes later, freshly showered, in nothing but a pair of jogging pants. His skin was slick, and I wanted to worship every inch of him with my tongue.

He took a seat at the table, and I rushed his coffee over to him. He took a sip and gave me a thumbs-up. I loaded the eggs and toast onto a plate and set it in front of him. When I went to move away, he wrapped an arm around my ass and pulled me close.

"Everything looks good, Joey," he praised, giving me a little pat on my butt.

"Thank you, sir." I grinned. "Was there anything else you needed?"

"Pepper," he said.

I quickly brought the pepper shaker to him, and he nodded, appeased. I made myself some toast and found some grape jelly in the fridge. I didn't really much care for eggs, so I poured myself a glass of OJ and sat down at the table. We ate in silence, and I watched as he went through the motions of eating his breakfast, every move elegant, using his napkin to blot his lips.

I knew I would love to do this every morning for him— prepare his food and watch as he savored my hard work. And then, if I were lucky, he'd kiss me or hold me a little for my efforts. And I wanted to be here when he got home, help him relax and pleasure him in whatever way he wanted me to that day. I wanted him to use me for his pleasure, spank me when I was naughty. I knew there was so much more to discover, and I wanted Gabriel to be my guide.

If ever there was a man worthy of being served, it was Gabriel. Despite his anger issues, he was a good person, and I felt proud to serve him.

I had been so caught up in my thoughts that I hadn't heard him call my name.

He chuckled. "Where did you go?"

"Ah…." I blushed and looked down at my half-eaten toast. "I was wondering if I could… talk to you about something."

When I looked back up, his brow was arched at me. "Finish your toast. Then collect all the dishes and put them where they belong. When you are done, come up to my office."

"Yes, sir."

Gabriel got up, then disappeared.

I wolfed my toast, poured the OJ down my throat, then collected everything into the sink. I stopped in the bathroom to gargle some mouthwash, then climbed the stairs to his office. I knocked, and he granted me entrance.

When I entered, I presented myself. Gabriel had a T-shirt on now, and his hair had been straightened, but he looked so relaxed. He pointed to the leather couch. "Get comfortable."

I bit my lip and settled onto the cushion. Gabriel came to join me, his body turned toward me, his elbow against the back.

"What did you want to talk about, Joey?" he inquired, his expression light, as if he were truly interested in hearing what I had to say.

Okay, so I knew what I wanted to say, but I stumbled for the correct words. Thinking and saying were two different things, I mused to myself. I took a deep breath. "Sir, I... I wanted to thank you for giving me this opportunity. You know... letting me serve you and everything. I really hope you enjoyed my time here too."

He nodded. "I have, Joey. Very much."

At his admission, I felt confidence fill me. "I thought about it a little bit yesterday, but it wasn't until this morning when I knew for sure that I... was *sure*. Even though this whole thing is still shocking to me, it feels *right*, and I really want to explore it more."

"Has there been a time at all when you thought you might not be able to do this?" he asked.

I cleared my throat. "You've done a lot of things that shocked me, but I think that's because it's all new to me, but... no, I never thought that."

"Not even when I was spanking you?" he asked, his tone getting a little dark, as if he'd enjoyed it.

I blushed, remembering every swing of that paddle. "Ah, no. I mean... it hurt, but it didn't really... scare me, I guess. And I so totally deserved it, and afterward when you held me, I felt so much better. Like… I had been cleansed. I don't know if that makes any sense."

"I completely understand what you are saying, and that is what you should feel. I'll be honest, I enjoyed spanking you, but the root of the punishment was to make amends for your mistakes and to wipe them clean," he said, getting closer. "Joey, was there any time when you felt things were moving a little too quickly?"

I took a few moments to think, replaying my time with him. "No, except… well, your room freaked me out a bit."

Gabriel's lips quirked up. "As I explained before, I will never force you to do something you're not comfortable with. That is why safewords are in place. I don't know your limits at all, but that is something that is to be discovered, especially with someone so new to the scene. My basement is more like a deep corner of my heart, the ultimate culmination of what I want in a relationship of this lifestyle. If this is going where I think it is, there may come a time when you so completely trust me, you won't hesitate to get on those things, but it can take a long time to get there, and if it scares you too much, then it won't happen."

I had needed to hear that, even if I already had. Sometimes you really needed to pound that square peg into the circular hole. "Thank you, sir."

"So, what are you saying, Joey?" Gabriel pushed.

"I… I want to… make this a permanent thing," I croaked, the excitement of possibility and the fear of the unknown parching my throat.

Gabriel smiled, and it was beautiful. "You want to sign a contract with me."

I took a deep breath. "Yes, sir. I do."

Gabriel was clearly delighted, his eyes on fire, and wow, I hadn't noticed that little dimple before. He got up and leaned over his desk, riffling through a drawer. When he returned to me, he had some papers in his hand. He handed them to me and sat back down.

"Read it," he said.

My eyes fell on the first few lines, and as I read the words, my mouth fell open.

Gabriel chuckled. "Read it out loud. We're going to discuss every line."

I licked my lips and cleared my throat. "The submissive will not be required to interact with animals of any kind in a sexual way, engage in scat or urination play or knife play, including drawing blood or being threatened with dangerous objects."

When I finished, I stared wide-eyed at Gabriel.

He chuckled. "There are those that enjoy such things. It's not for me to judge, but I have no desire to experience it, so you're safe."

Deciding to leave that one alone—I'd have time to contemplate the weirdness of human sexuality later—I went on. "The submissive will fully belong to the Master. He will not engage in any sexual activity with anyone and will not be required to pleasure third parties either with hand, mouth, or asshole. Masturbation, unless ordered, is strictly prohibited, and any violations will be swiftly and severely corrected. The submissive is not required to alter his body with piercings, tattoos, or brands; however, should the submissive wish to modify his body, the issue will be thoroughly discussed, and if both parties agree, shall be carried out by a professional."

I looked at Gabriel, trying to imagine his initials somewhere on my body—maybe on my ass, or in a more intimate corner—maybe on my scrotum where no one but Gabriel would see.

"Joey? You understand that?" Gabriel inquired.

"Yes, sir. If I wanted to get a piercing, I could, though?"

That quirk returned to his lips. "I bet you'd look hot with a cock ring."

I cringed. "That sounds… painful."

He chuckled and motioned to the papers in my hands. I started reading again. "The duty of the submissive: The Master reserves the right to use the submissive in any way he wishes whenever he chooses, day or night, public or private. The submissive's hands, mouth, tongue, nipples, cock, balls, and asshole are the property of the Master, as well as the submissive's orgasms. The submissive should be respectful at all times and refer to the Master as Sir. The submissive will be required to follow the Master's instructions quickly and efficiently and with pride. The submissive should be grateful when a punishment is dealt and holds the right to cry, scream, beg, and curse, but the Master reserves the right to gag the submissive if he desires. The submissive will not attempt to avoid a punishment, including lying about an infraction, or physically stop the punishment from being carried out. The submissive will understand that the Master will never issue a punishment for the sake of punishing. The submissive will understand that a punishment is necessary and will become routine in the early stages of the newly formed relationship until the submissive is familiar with the Master's expectations. Should the submissive find that he enjoys a particular punishment, the submissive will inform the Master immediately, and a different punishment will be enacted so that punishment does not become reward."

"Stop," Gabriel interrupted. "Did you understand everything that you've read? Particularly the last part. Since you've had very little experience, you don't quite know what you like yet. Tell me, Joey, was there a moment, even a second, that you enjoyed me spanking you?"

I bit my lip in thought. I nodded, my cheeks flaming. "It was… kinda nice at first, but then it just hurt. And I had liked when you spanked me with your crop."

Gabriel nodded, pleased. "There are a lot of people that enjoy the pain something like that brings. A little spanking can feel nice, but what I am talking about is true pain, like you had experienced with my paddle. Did it at any time arouse you?"

I frowned. "No, sir."

Gabriel stroked his chin. "I want you to know you shouldn't be ashamed if experiencing pain turns you on. Did you know pleasure and pain travel along the same receptors? Anyway, the point I'm trying to make is that you don't know who you are yet and that should you discover a particular pain arouses you, I need you to inform me right away. Punishment is not punishment if it becomes reward, and vice versa. Do you understand what I am telling you, Joey?"

"Yes, sir, I do." I nodded. "If I had liked to be spanked like that you would use it as a reward instead?"

"Good boy. That's absolutely right." He smiled. "Continue on."

"Acceptable punishments may include but are not limited to spanking, orgasm denial, written essays, standing in the corner, restriction of privileges, cock and ball torture—" I swallowed hard, my throat tight, but managed to go on. "—high-retention enemas, binding, and short-term solitude—"

"Stop," he said sharply. "Come with me."

I followed, my knees weak. He took a seat at his desk and pulled me in so that I was sitting on his leg. He wrapped an arm around me, pulling me close. I watched as he opened his laptop and brought up the digital format of the contract.

"We're going to make some amendments specifically for you," Gabriel explained. "I'm going to talk; you're going to type. Under the punishment clause, in parentheses, add this: The Master will not blindfold, mask, lock in dark rooms, boxes, or any small spaces. The Master will not use any fears or phobias against the submissive."

I started typing the words, my hands shaky. I felt tears prick my eyes that Gabriel would be so kind in that regard. I felt him press his lips to my shoulder, planting a soft kiss, letting me know everything was okay. When I was done, I waited.

"Anything else you might like to add to that?" Gabriel inquired.

"Ah... no I think that's.... C-cock and ball t-torture?" I stuttered.

He chuckled softly. "Does that scare you, Joey?"

"Well... yes. I mean, wouldn't it scare most men?" I poked, glad I could joke with him.

"Some like it. As I said before, anything you're not ready for yet, you let me know. Think of these next few months as school.... Anyway, continue on where you left off."

"Breath control is optional, and the Master will not punish the submissive should the submissive wish to opt out." I glanced at Gabriel. "Sir?"

He took a deep breath and closed his eyes for a moment. "Breath control is one of the highest forms of trust, Joey. It is something I would like to explore, but have not yet had a submissive hold such trust in me. As the contract states, it is optional for both parties."

I nodded and went on. "Any other punishments, rewards, or acts may be explored on both parties' wishes, but the submissive holds the right to opt out and amend the contract should he find that said act encroaches his hard limit. The submissive holds the right to use his safeword but agrees not to abuse it in order to get out of a punishment. Conduct expectations: The submissive should always address the Master with a polite, respectful tone and offer the Master his full attention. The submissive promises to share any reservations or feelings he may be having at any time, whether in the middle of punishment or reward. The submissive promises to communicate with the Master without fear of punishment. The submissive will be required to keep a tally of his transgressions and record them into a book...." I went on, reading the details about the points book Gabriel had explained to me.

"The submissive will be required to keep regular contact with the Master while not under the Master's care, including phone, text, or video feed. The submissive consents to being photographed or videotaped in any way, shape, or form, and the Master promises that all videos and photographs will be destroyed upon termination of contract if the submissive requests. The submissive will be responsible for carrying out chores, tasks, and errands as the Master so declares. It will be the submissive's duty to tend to the Master in all ways including but not limited to bathing, grooming, dressing, preparing meals, massages, and any other activities to relax the Master. The submissive will be responsible for cleaning and maintaining all sex toys."

I took a deep breath and licked my lips, my mouth dry. Gabriel chuckled and said against my skin, "Go on downstairs and get a bottle of water."

"Yes, sir," I said, and bolted for the door. I closed it softly behind me and entered the kitchen, snatching a cool bottle of mountain water. I made a move to crack the lid but stopped. Gabriel might want some too.

When I was granted permission back into his office, he was still at his chair, but there were two glasses on the desk. I made a move to present, but he motioned for me to join him. Gabriel pulled me back into his lap, then split the bottle of water between us. I gulped my share down.

He chuckled. "Continue on."

I cleared my throat and started reading again. "It will be the submissive's duty to maintain his body in the way the Master wishes. While in privacy, the submissive will not be allowed clothes and will ensure that his body is easily accessible at all times. The submissive agrees to wear at all times that this contract is valid a token of his possession, given to him by the Master. The role of the Master: The Master promises to—"

Gabriel cut me off. "The Master promises to accept responsibility for the submissive's body as I see fit under the provisions of this contract. I promise to care for the submissive, to hold his well-being, both physical and emotional, and safety above all else as long as this contract is valid. I promise to respect the submissive, train him, and instruct him to my wishes, to punish him and care for him as I see fit."

I zoned out on the screen, but I didn't need to see the words to know Gabriel was reciting the contract word for word without reading from it. He touched my chin, urging me to look at him. I shifted on his lap and looked into those beautiful silver eyes as he went on.

"I promise I will listen to all of the submissive's concerns and discuss any issues. I promise never to reprimand or punish the submissive for asking questions. I promise I will respect the submissive's safewords and cease any and all actions. I will not take the submissive's basic necessities of eating, drinking, sleeping, or using the bathroom away for amusement or punishment. I will respect the submissive's family life and promise not to interfere with school, work, or social responsibility. I will hold the submissive's role detailed in this contract in confidentiality. I will respect the submissive's right at any time to amend or cancel this contract."

Gabriel smiled at me, his eyes glowing as he ran his thumb across my back. I couldn't speak, could hardly breathe. It was as if he were vowing himself to me and I to him.

"Anything else you want to add?" he inquired.

I gaped for a moment, my mind mush. "Ah... I was hoping that maybe... we could, um, explore my fantasies?"

He nodded and pointed to the laptop. "Under the Master's role provision, type in parentheses: 'The Master promises to explore the submissive's fantasies in full as he sees fit.'"

I did as instructed, my stomach churning. Gabriel made me go through the entire contract again, making sure I understood everything. As I read it out loud, he held me tenderly, his lips pressed to my shoulder, his fingers securing me firmly to him. The intimacy of the moment shocked me. It was like an all-new high, discussing our roles. What really made my day was Gabriel's concern for my safety. It made me trust him.

"Print it," he said when we were done.

I hit the print button, and the printer started whirling, spitting out pages. Gabriel retrieved the contract and laid it on the desk. He flipped to the last page and signed his name, then dated it. He offered me the pen, and I took it with a shaky hand. I looked at his signature on the line—it was so elegant and flowing. I signed my own name.

Gabriel sucked at my earlobe and growled. "You are now mine."

My cock jerked, and I heard myself moan. I wanted to be owned by this man, possessed. I wanted to serve and pleasure him. I managed to whisper, "I'm yours, sir."

"Collect the papers and make copies," he said, pointing at the combo machine to the side.

"Yes, sir."

I did as instructed, placing each of the papers on the glass and copying them. Gabriel had come up behind me and touched my ass, his palms running all over as if he were savoring what might be coming very soon. As I worked on copying the contract, he kissed my behind and stroked my thighs until I was hard.

I managed to collect myself to hand him the papers.

"The original signed contract will stay with you. I'll take the copy." He accepted the contract, then swiveled around to his safe and unlocked it. He withdrew a manila folder and placed the papers in between, then set the folder back inside. "Present yourself to me on the rug."

"Yes, sir." I didn't hesitate, taking position in the middle of the room on the Aubusson rug.

I waited as he worked behind his desk. I couldn't see what he was doing and was anxious to know. Finally, he got up and came around to join me, something in his hand. He cradled it in his palms, his fingers stroking the black nylon. It was a collar of sorts.

"I bought this just the other day in anticipation that you'd sign a contract. It is a training collar, Joey. Its low quality and simplicity signifies your inexperience and roughness. Only when I decide you are ready will you graduate and receive a true slave's collar," he said, coming to kneel down next to me.

I couldn't help but gape as he slid it around my neck, then adjusted the buckle.

"Too tight?" he asked.

"No, sir." It felt just right, not tight but not loose.

He reached in his pocket and produced a tiny lock and a key hanging from a necklace. As he secured the collar, he explained, "The only way the collar will be removed is in a medical emergency, if the contract is voided, or when you graduate."

"Yes, sir," I said breathlessly.

I watched as he slipped the chain and key around his neck. The collar felt heavy, the fabric soft, and it felt... *right*.

"Now, get dressed." He grinned. "You're going to need some toys."

What?

I COULDN'T stop looking at Gabriel as he drove, his face light, his attention on the road. I was *his*. It was a concept that hadn't completely sunk in yet, but I couldn't wait to explore it further.

We'd been on the road for about twenty minutes, driving farther north so that the cityscape was no longer visible behind us. Gabriel had said toys, but I had no idea where he was taking me. Eventually, we pulled into a parking lot at what looked like a miniwarehouse of sorts.

I followed behind him as he led me toward the entrance. When we stepped inside, I gasped. "Toys" was right. There were so many things that I couldn't comprehend what I was seeing. Leather and whips, chains and paddles... dildos of all shapes and sizes. Things I had absolutely no name for. I flushed when I got a look at a mask with a dong protruding from the mouth.

Gabriel threw an arm around my shoulders and led me farther into the "toy store." There was an elderly woman of about sixty at a counter, her gray hair cut into a pageboy. She turned to us and held out her arms, her eyes bright. My eyes immediately fell to the collar around her neck.

Gabriel embraced her. "Nice to see you again, Martha."

"Likewise, Mr. Mason." She said, then turned to me. "Is this yours?"

Gabriel regarded me, something twinkling in his eyes. "Indeed."

"Handsome. Young." She smiled becomingly. "Let me know if you need help with anything."

"Will do. How is Dwayne, by the way?" Gabriel inquired.

"Wonderful, thank you. His annual checkup was clear," she said, tipping her head. "I will tell him you said hello."

I watched as the woman went back to whatever she was doing. I heard Gabriel chuckle, but I was so caught up in everything that my attention was pulled ten different ways.

"Joey?"

"Yes, sir?" I asked, my attention on some sort of leather thong—it didn't look very comfortable.

"Grab a cart over there," he said, motioning to the side.

"Yes, sir." I did as instructed, my eyes darting everywhere. This place was crazy… crazy good. I couldn't help but ask, "Is she a… slave?"

"Yes. Martha and Dwayne have been involved longer than I've been on this earth." He smiled as if he were recalling pleasant memories. "It was Dwayne who introduced me to the life, showed me how to express my desires. You're going to meet a lot of fascinating people in this lifestyle. Young and old, gay or straight, we're a colorful mix."

I followed Gabriel down the aisles as he inspected items, swung a rubber paddle in the air as if imagining himself using it on me. He made a sound of delight, and I followed him toward one of the walls, where there was a display case of… dildos.

I swallowed hard as he examined them, his lips pulled up into a sly smirk. He motioned to Martha, and she approached. Gabriel started reading off codes, my eyes frantically trying to match them to the correct dong.

"I'll be right back," she said and disappeared.

I followed Gabriel and watched uneasily as he tossed things into the cart. I tried to keep my cool, but some of the things he had chosen were intimidating—leather cuffs and anklets and a cock cuff? Though some of the stuff he had tossed in the cart scared me, I trusted that he would take care in introducing me to everything.

Martha returned some time later, her arms filled with packaged dongs. She set them in the cart, and I blanched. They were all sizes, some small, others... huge. I had no idea how the aptly labeled "Monster Dong" would fit in me, and I was sure my eyes had popped out of my sockets. There was a purple dildo that had some sort of spikes all over it.

Gabriel simply laughed darkly. I had plastered my hands to the cart as I followed him, feeling as if my limbs might be ripped off if they got in the way of anything. It was like a walk through a haunted house—scary, but thrilling nonetheless. I sighed as I eyed the spiky purple dildo he had chosen. I was sure I could expect it to be used in some sort of punishment.

Gabriel stopped and peered into a display case, and I looked at what I believed were cock cages. Some were simple plastic like *It* had been wearing, others metal and wire, but none looked particularly comfortable. Okay, the human imagination was really something. I never would have thought chastity belts for men existed.

"Do you think you have fairly decent self-control, Joey?" Gabriel asked, his attention on the glass case.

"Ah... I suppose so." I stumbled.

"I'll never order you to do something you are incapable of doing. I know how it is at your age. I went through the same thing. I'm going to pass on the cage for now, but if you ever feel that you are unable to keep yourself from masturbating, you will inform me immediately, and I will take measures to prevent you from doing so.

As I said before, you are only allowed to come when I say you can," he explained.

"Yes, sir," I acknowledged, and looked askance at the cock cages. But Gabriel's thoughtfulness put me at ease. The last thing I wanted to do was disappoint him.

By the time we got home, it was well past noon, and I helped Gabriel carry my new toys into the house, stopping only to remove my shoes. We lugged everything into the "toy room." Gabriel started going through all the bags, removing the dildos from the packaging and having me set them in the cabinets according to his precise instructions. We arranged them so that they ran from smallest to largest. When he handed me that Monster Dong, I wiggled it in my hands, completely freaked out by it. I couldn't imagine myself ever taking such a large object. I supposed only time would tell.

Once the dildos where settled in their new homes, the plugs were next. Gabriel moved on to some cock rings and cuffs, and I watched as he put everything away. He was having fun; his expression was light and his eyes were glowing. I couldn't help but smile. Though I had only spent a few days with him, I had come to realize he was a very caring man, and it must have hurt him when his previous submissive passed away. I wanted to ask what had happened, but I didn't feel as if it were my place. Maybe after we got to know each other better and grew closer, I would ask.

When everything was settled, I began collecting the boxes and bags into one pile. I noticed there was a small plug lying in one, and retrieved it. He must have missed it. I made a move to reunite it with its friends, but Gabriel stopped me.

"No, that's different," he said, then commanded I follow with the plug.

He led me into his bedroom, then pointed to the bedside table, where a small silk cloth was folded. "Set it there."

I did as told, not understanding the significance of his request, but whatever he wanted, I'd do. Gabriel came up behind me and wrapped his arms around my body.

His voice was husky. "Do you understand what it means?"

"No, sir," I answered. I thought maybe he wanted something close by, should he desire to play with me in the middle of the night or… something.

His voice was wicked against my ear, his breath hot. "From now on I will only come in your mouth or your ass. I am a firm believer in safe sex, but there may come a time when you trust me enough to allow the latter. This is wholly your choice, but when and if it happens, well, I think you get the point."

I swallowed hard, suddenly feeling hot. My mind flashed with images of the future, Gabriel buried deep inside me. I could see his body tighten, a vicious snarl ripped from his lips as he spilled into me. Then he was pushing the plug in my ass to keep his semen from spilling out.

It got hot, really hot, really quickly. I heard him chuckle against my ear. He started loosening my clothes, pushing my shirt over my head. Then my pants were falling down my legs. I stepped out, pushing them away. His arms came around me, holding me securely to him, and I had to fight to keep my hands from reaching for him.

He licked at my earlobe. "You're mine now, Joey. Do you know what that means?"

I did, but I wanted to hear him say it anyway.

"I'm going to fuck you now," he growled, then bent me over the bed.

My breath left me in a huff, his words burrowing deep into me, lighting me up. Then his hands were on my ass, my hips, my back, until I couldn't tell where he ended. I felt his cock press against my ass through his pants, the jeans rasping against my skin.

"Please…," I begged desperately. "Please, sir…."

He seemed delighted. "Get on the bed."

I obeyed and watched as he lifted his shirt over his head and unhooked his jeans. He discarded his clothes haphazardly, then came to join me in the bed. My heart was pounding, my stomach a tumble of nerves. He pulled me close and wrapped me up in his heat, his fingers stroking me. I dug my fingers into my own skin.

"Do you understand why you must have permission to touch me, Joey?" he inquired.

I opened my mouth and thought for a moment. He was watching me with curious eyes, his face relaxed—I knew he was letting me work this out for myself. "Because you, ah... want to control me?"

"Half-right." He smiled faintly. "I want you to know what your body is doing at all times, but also because total submission demands that everything you do is for my benefit. You touching me of your own volition is fulfilling *your* desire. It's important that you learn to control yourself so that you can respond quickly and efficiently when I give an order. Do you understand what I am saying?"

I absorbed all that he had said. Now that he explained it to me, it made total sense. Any other day, I didn't hesitate to touch something—whether it be Aunt Hanny or a bottle of soda—because it was what I wanted to do. "Yes, sir."

"As time goes on and we learn each other more, I will eventually demolish that rule, and you will have learned to anticipate when and how I want you to touch me." Gabriel planted a kiss on my cheek. He grinned and whispered softly, "Right now, I'm giving you permission to touch me in whatever way you want. Are you ready for me, slave?"

"Yes, sir," I managed, my voice hoarse.

He gripped my ass and ran his fingers up my crack, grazing my asshole. I couldn't help but pant as he explored me, teasing my entrance with his finger. "Did you clean yourself this morning?"

"Yes, sir... I... I was hoping you would... after I decided...." I could barely speak, but Gabriel seemed to understand, because he grinned.

He left me quickly, and I almost whimpered, but when I saw he had retrieved a tube of lube and a condom from the nightstand, I bit my lip. He spread some lube on his fingers, then returned to me, smearing the moisture up and down my crack. When a finger probed my ass, I gasped. He finger fucked me with that single digit, driving me wild with need. I wanted more. I wanted his big cock inside of me, taking his pleasure.

Another finger slipped in, and I gasped, the intrusion stretching me. I couldn't describe what I was feeling—I just felt soooo good, but I needed more. He withdrew from me and rolled onto his back. I watched in astonishment as he rolled the condom over his cock, then squirted a little more lube in his hand.

"Turn on your other side," Gabriel commanded.

I did as bade, and he came up against me. He positioned me so that I was comfortable, his bicep acting as my pillow, my ass flush against his pelvic cradle. He pushed my leg forward so I was open for him, and then I felt his glans press against my entrance. I took a deep breath to steady myself and forced myself to relax. I'd been waiting for this for a long time—okay, so three weeks weren't that long, but I really wanted to have a man inside me.

I gasped as Gabriel entered me, the head of his cock slipping past the muscles of my asshole. He didn't proceed any further, giving me a moment to get used to him. It didn't hurt but felt weird. He was bigger than the dildos he had used on me, and I couldn't help but be a little taken aback by what was happening.

His palm stroked up my abdomen as he pushed a little more, my ass loosening, accepting him. As he slid into me, I groaned, feeling filled to capacity—but God, it was amazing.

"How is this?" he inquired, his voice hoarse.

"So good, sir… thank you…." I moaned softly as he went as deep as he could go.

I dug my fingers into the sheets as Gabriel held me securely, his cock buried in my ass. I let him support me as he slowly fucked me, each stroke driving me crazy. I felt his lips press against the back of my neck, his arm lift my leg up. He increased his pace, the constant, fluid stimulation making my cock jerk. On some level I couldn't believe this was happening, that a cock was in my ass, pumping me, and that was part of the thrill. Caught up by everything that was happening, I laid voice to my pleasure.

"That's it, Joey," he purred against my ear. "Let me hear you—don't even think of holding back."

I wanted to respond, but when Gabriel thrust deep into me I barked out a groan. He was pleased, growling as he sucked at the skin of my shoulder until it hurt. I wasn't sure when I had lost track of time and reality. All I knew was Gabriel, his veiny cock working me good so that I could barely stand the pleasure, it was so intense.

I heard him curse, and his strokes slowed. He laughed in my ear. "Fucking hell… you feel too good."

I moaned softly and flexed my muscles. He landed a hard spank on my ass, and I gasped.

"Trying to make me lose control? Naughty slave," he teased.

I moaned an affirmative, smiling against his arm. His cock left me, and I whimpered, but I was pushed onto my stomach roughly.

"Offer yourself," he hissed.

I obeyed, getting on my knees and spreading my ass cheeks. He came against me in an instant, his cock penetrating me. He was able to go deeper this way, and I groaned as he filled me even more. He started fucking me again in slow, long thrusts, and it wasn't long before my body started jerking as he hit something deep inside.

"Stroke yourself," he commanded hoarsely.

"Yes… sir," I managed and gripped my cock, my other hand still spreading myself. I forced myself to go slow. I knew it wouldn't be long until I was ready to come, and Gabriel hadn't given me permission yet. As I worked my dick, my insides tightened, and I was unable to keep myself from squeezing my muscles—it just felt so much better that way….

Gabriel barked a vicious curse and pulled away. He snapped the condom off and growled, "Come over here and accept your master's cum."

I didn't hesitate, my limbs weak as I scrambled to him. When I got close, he pushed me onto my back so that his cock was right above me. I extended my tongue in preparation. He slapped his cock against my cheek, his eyes bright, his expression tense. I could see that he was frustrated about something, but I didn't ask, just let him use me as he wished.

"I didn't tell you to stop stroking yourself," he said harshly.

"Sorry, sir," I sputtered and gripped my cock.

He tapped my tongue with his glans, and I instinctively licked at the underside until he groaned. I knew he liked it like that, and I didn't hesitate to exploit it. I watched him as his body tightened, and when he threw his head back, I knew what was coming. I opened my mouth as far as my jaw would allow. He came into my mouth on a roar, filling me in a different way, and I couldn't help but smile.

He asked dazedly. "You think it's funny to make me lose control, slave?"

I shook my head, unable to speak. He laughed wickedly, then commanded me to swallow. I obeyed.

"No, sir, I'm just happy I could pleasure you," I managed, my own orgasm quickly building.

"Uh-huh," he teased, then leaned over me so that his balls were in my face. I followed my gut and licked at the smooth skin, his manly scent heavy in my nose. "That's right, worship your master."

I mumbled against his skin, licking and sucking. I felt one of my legs being drawn back behind his arm so that my hole was exposed, and when he thrust his fingers into my ass, I gasped and groaned against him. He started fucking me in quick, hard thrusts that were both uncomfortable and pleasurable.

"Come," he ordered.

I made indecipherable sounds against his sac as he hit something inside me. Between his balls in my mouth and his fingers in my ass, I was delirious as the orgasm shot out of me, splattering all over my stomach. I voiced my pleasure against his scrotum, and he didn't stop thrusting until every last drop was wrung from my cock.

"Please, sir…," I mumbled.

Gabriel laughed, and I knew he had that wolfish grin on his lips. "What are you begging me for?"

I had no clue. I simply lolled my head and went back to licking his balls. My cock was still in my hand, rock hard. He didn't remove his fingers from my ass, instead slowly massaged me, and I wiggled from the stimulation. The sensation was ridiculously intense, almost uncomfortable, but as another orgasm coiled in my balls, I gasped against his sac.

I heard Gabriel remark, "The benefits of youth. Although it can be a punishment too. I once milked a boy's prostate until he was brought to tears. When I was done, he resembled an iced donut."

His words startled me a little, but the pleasure clouded everything over. "Sir…," I gasped. "Can… I…?"

"You may come," he said.

I licked and sucked at him with renewed vigor as I pumped my aching cock, his fingers working inside me. The second orgasm came out of nowhere, and I cried against his nut sac, the explosion wracking my body. As the orgasm subsided, his thrusts slowed, until finally my ass was vacated. He moved away from me and left me on the bed, a puddle. My cock was still throbbing, my ass felt sore and empty, and… I couldn't even move, much less breathe.

I wasn't sure where Gabriel had gone, but he quickly shot into view and came to sit down beside me. He wiped the mess on my stomach with a washcloth.

He chuckled. "You've soiled my bed."

"Sorry… sir," I managed.

He didn't respond, instead whacked my cock with the cloth. I gasped from the pain and searched his face. He was smiling. I returned his happiness, and then I was being drawn to him, my body limp in his arms. He settled me against him, my head against his shoulder. He took my hand and pressed my palm against his chest.

I thought I would burst from joy as he planted a kiss on my forehead. "Good slave, you've made your master happy."

Eleven

I SIGHED in contentment and grabbed onto Gabriel as my eyes fluttered open. I hadn't realized I'd fallen asleep. I felt his fingers stroke my hair, the touch soothing. His body was so warm and soft and hard at the same time.... I never wanted to move.

"Welcome back, slave," Gabriel purred.

I smiled against his chest. "Thank you, sir."

We lay like this for a while, Gabriel touching me softly, my cheek pressed to his chest so that I could hear his heart beating. My body was a little stiff, sore from being well used, but it was a truly wonderful feeling. There was something to be said about just being with someone after great sex. It went past the physical, and I felt as if we had connected on some level.

"How do you feel?" he inquired, his voice husky.

I couldn't help but grin like a fool. "Amazing."

"Good," he rumbled. "Looking forward to tomorrow?"

Wow, I had almost forgotten. Gabriel had commanded all my attention. Now that I remembered tomorrow was my first day of college, I sighed wistfully. "Yes, sir, I am, but... I'm conflicted."

"Talk to me," he ordered.

"I want to stay here with you, be here in the morning for you, but I—can't wait for tomorrow."

His fingers ran down my shoulder, making me shiver. "I would like for you to be here, but school is important. I want you to be the best you can be, both in serving me and academically. It would fill me with pride to watch you come into your own. Can you imagine the bragging rights I'll be entitled to should you become a best-selling novelist?"

"Thank you, sir." I beamed.

He chuckled softly before saying, "Besides, I've been thinking. The weekends are not enough. Your training is going to intensify, and I think it would be better if you spent more time with me. You said your classes are done by four?"

"Yes. Noon to four," I said in confirmation. I so wanted to spend more time with Gabriel.

"If you can make it to O'Hare, I can pick you up from there. I figure as long as I get you back by ten, you should be good," he said.

"I think that's a good idea, sir." I nodded.

"We'll do it Tuesday and Thursday. But, Joey... if your time with me interferes with your schoolwork, you will let me know," he commanded, his tone harsh, letting me know it wasn't up for debate.

"Yes, sir. I promise, sir."

"Good boy," he whispered and patted my butt.

He got up and headed for the bathroom. I collapsed against the sheets warmed by our bodies. I had never before felt so... right, so... *complete*. I remembered what Gabriel had told me about finally finding himself and coming to terms with who he was. I could safely say I now understood that feeling intimately. There was still a lot I didn't know, but I was looking forward to exploring it with Gabriel.

I listened as the water came on and the toilet flushed. I had no idea what was going to happen from this point on, and that was part of the thrill. Gabriel was here to guide me, though, and I knew I was in good hands.

When he emerged from the bathroom, he said, "You have five minutes to collect yourself. Then I expect you in my office."

"Yes, sir," I confirmed, and watched as he left the room.

I took a deep breath and slowly let it out, the scent of Gabriel and sex heavy in the room. I dragged my feet into the bathroom, then relieved myself. As I washed my hands, I caught my reflection. It was strange, but I looked as if I'd aged a few years during these past few weeks. Physically, I looked the same—plain brown hair, blue eyes, great skin—but it wasn't something I could completely describe. I felt it, though, felt the youth leaving me. I was no longer a kid, but a man.

I smiled like an idiot at my reflection, then finished up in the bathroom. When I was granted access to his office, I presented myself and waited. Gabriel was staring down at a piece of paper, his brows furrowed, his lips tight. Eventually, he shoved it away, then reached into his desk.

"Come here," he ordered.

I got to my feet and came to join him behind his desk. He pulled me into his lap, his arms going around my waist.

"Have you ever kept a diary, Joey?" he inquired.

"Ah… no, sir." I fumbled to explain. "Not in the conventional sense."

He made a sound of acknowledgment and handed me a small book. It was the same size as my points book, but this one was bound in white leather.

"I want you to write down your thoughts concerning our relationship. I will never read nor ask you to read from the book. Whatever you write is solely for you. It will be one of the very few things that you own," he said. "I didn't have an outlet for the things I was going through when I was a kid. I just sort of bottled everything up, and when it came out, things got smashed. I don't want that for you. And if there is something you want me to know, I want you to tell me without fear of embarrassment, but your private thoughts are your own."

"Thank you, sir," I whispered, caught off guard by Gabriel's concern for my well-being.

He kissed my shoulder. "If ever there is a time that you have reservations about our relationship, I want you to let me know. There is a reason I gave you the original contract. Study it until it's branded in your mind. It is not just your pledge to me, but also my promise to you."

"Yes, sir," I croaked, running my fingers along the bumpy leather.

"Also… you should know there may be times when you will not be allowed to come for a while. It all depends on my mood, really. I was easy on you this week, but things are going to intensify in the coming months. Should you feel the urge to masturbate, I want you to call me right away. You are under no circumstances allowed to come without my permission, and if you think you can't control yourself, I will take measures to ensure that it doesn't happen. The last thing I want for you is to break your word—and I don't need to tell you how shitty you will feel by lying to me if you have. I'll train you to control your orgasms, but that takes time. *Capisce*?"

"Yes, sir. Thank you, sir." I swallowed hard at his words. They excited me and at the same time scared me. I was afraid I'd cave in to the physical urge, but I didn't know if I had the resolution to confess it to him. His words made sense, though. I would indeed feel like crap for lying to him.

"What else… what else…," he whispered. "Do you have any questions?"

"Ah…. No, I don't think so," I admitted.

"Oh! I'm giving you another writing assignment—it is not a punishment. When Saturday comes, you will have ready for me a list of ten things you want in your life—dreams or goals pertaining to this relationship or outside. After that you will name ten things that scare you—phobias or otherwise."

"Yes, sir."

"Hm, okay, well, it's late, and we need to get you back soon. I want you to have time for yourself tonight. You should be well rested for your first day," he said. "Go run us a bath in the hot tub. Fill it only halfway. The water should be hot but not scorching."

"Yes, sir," I confirmed, and exited the office.

I did as instructed. As the tub filled, I took the liberty of setting two big towels on the sink counter. Gabriel came to join me and stepped in, hissing at the warmth of the water. At first I thought I had made it too hot, but he got in and groaned in contentment, a smile on his lips. He hit a button on the side, and the jets kicked in, rustling the water.

"Come attend your master, slave," he growled.

"Yes, sir." I smiled and joined him. The water was a little hot for my tastes, but I reminded myself this wasn't for me. Besides, the bubbles from the rushing water felt good against my body. I was a little stiff in places, and if I were lucky, the warmth and motion of the water would loosen me up.

With his eyes closed, he pointed to the wall. "The apricot scrub and sponge."

I slid over to the wall and retrieved the bottle and sponge. I squirted some onto the sponge, then worked it into a nice froth. I ran the scrubber across Gabriel's chest, and he sighed. I was mesmerized by the way the suds coated his body, sliding down his slick skin. I couldn't help but wish I had pecs like he did. I promised myself I would work on that. I wanted to be the best I could for this amazing man.

"Good boy," he mumbled.

I smiled like a fool as I washed him, running the sponge all over his body. He propped a leg up on the side of the tub, and I didn't hesitate. My fingers found a line of risen flesh—the scar I had noticed earlier.

"Can I ask a question, sir?"

Apparently, Gabriel knew what I was going to ask, because he said, "Broke my kneecap when I was a kid, tore some ligaments too. Had to have a few surgeries. Not too big of a deal, but it seems age is catching up with me—damn arthritis."

I wanted to ask more but decided I would have time later. When I got to his foot, he hissed.

"Sorry, sir?"

His lips quirked up. "Ticklish."

Oh, how… adorable.

"You think that's funny, slave?" he inquired, his tone thick with amusement.

"No, sir," I answered honestly. "It… ah… it endears you to me more."

I jerked as sly fingers wormed across my belly, my smile making my cheeks hurt.

He laughed, pleased. "Good to know. You try to exploit it, and you'll be sorry. There's nothing in our contract excluding tickle torture. I swear, I won't stop until you piss yourself."

I swallowed hard. His tone was light, but I knew he was serious.

When I was done soaping him up, he curled his finger toward him, and I obeyed. He pulled me into him so that I was straddling his hips. He took the sponge from me and ran it up and down my back. The abrasive surface felt good. His hands explored me, running everywhere, dipping into my crack. He pushed at my entrance, and I gasped.

"I can't wait to fuck you again," he whispered.

"You can take me now, sir. I am yours," I managed.

He clearly liked my words, because he smiled like a wolf. I thought he was going to back off, tell me that we didn't have the time, but as his finger penetrated me, I groaned.

"Are you sore at all?" he inquired, watching me closely.

"Good sore, sir." I smiled. "In fact, I can take you now—"

He laughed darkly. "You'll get me when I am ready, slave— many, many times."

He forced another digit in, and I moaned. The stretching was good, but I now more keenly felt the effect of being used. I wanted to touch him but managed to grip the edge of the tub behind him instead. He finger fucked me for a little, my cock hardening from the stimulation. I still wanted him inside me.

"I'm speaking honestly, but there will be times when you don't want me, when you may be sore from prior use. Though I will be considerate, I will still take you whenever I wish, slave. Now that you've been broken in, I won't hesitate to use this hole."

His words shattered me in a good way, and I gasped, "Yes, sir."

Just like that, he left me, my ass feeling empty. The sponge started working over me again, and I whimpered, my cock needing attention.

Gabriel chuckled. "Did I not tell you, you will come only when I say you can?"

"Yes, sir."

He grinned and let the sponge fall into the water. Then he slid below the surface. I watched, transfixed, as he reemerged, his hair plastered to his forehead, the soap rinsed away.

"Rinse yourself. Then retrieve the towels."

"Yes, sir," I confirmed and imitated his movement, only to get a mouthful of water. I choked and turned away in embarrassment.

Gabriel pulled me into him roughly, his voice a purr in my ear. "Clumsy slave. It endears you to me."

I smiled shyly at his tone. It was both mocking and playful. He sucked my earlobe in, and I moaned softly. Just like that, he let me go, and I got out of the water. I took one of the towels and quickly dried myself, then held out the other for him. Gabriel got out, and I wrapped him up in the massive towel.

"I'm going to renegotiate the rules a little concerning touching me. You will be allowed to touch me benignly while taking a bath, sleeping with me, or any other way that requires you to assist me, such as dressing. However, attempting to arouse me during these situations will be met with punishment. I decide when and how you will service me. Understand?"

"Yes, sir," I said with enthusiasm.

"Good boy. Release the water and make sure that everything is nice and tidy. Then get dressed. We're going to get some food before I take you back home," he instructed, strutting into the bedroom.

My eyes were on his ass as I acknowledged his order, a big, goofy grin on my lips.

BY THE time we pulled up to my house, it was almost nine. Gabriel had taken us to a little hot dog place. I'd ordered a Chicago dog, and he had ordered a plain chicken sandwich. The mood had been light, and Gabriel had rehashed some of the details of our contract, most notably my promise to communicate with him. By his voice, I could tell he was as excited as I was about our new relationship.

The drive back to my neighborhood was mostly quiet, the mild spring air blowing in our faces as Gabriel took control of the road and everyone on it. Some guy had given us the finger, and Gabriel had spewed obscene things out the window at him. Gabriel was a very aggressive man, and that fact made me feel safe, that he'd protect me in this new world. It also worried me. I was afraid I'd do something, and he'd blow up. But the way he'd handled my big omission set me at ease. He might have a temper, but I got the sense that he was in control of it just like he was in control of everything else.

I turned my attention to my modest place of residence, the house not even half the size of Gabriel's pad. I still wondered how I'd gotten here, in this awesome car with such an amazing man.

"Joey?"

I regarded him. "Yes, sir?"

"I expect you in bed early tonight. Get a good night's sleep, and don't daydream about my cock through your classes tomorrow."

I flushed and laughed at myself. "Yes, sir."

His fingers were warm as he forced me to look at him. "I'll be expecting a call from you once you get home. I'd like to know how everything went."

"Yes, sir."

"Good boy." He nodded toward his door and got out.

I followed. Just as I managed to close the car door, he came up behind me. I turned to regard him, and he pushed me against the car, his body caging me in. He set his hands on the hood behind me and pressed his hips into mine. I looked at him with wide eyes, and his lips quirked up. I watched as he came so close that I could see the evening stubble on his jaw. His lips parted, and I subconsciously leaned in.

Gabriel backed away just a little. "Are you demanding something of me, slave?"

"N-no, sir," I whispered hoarsely.

"Close your eyes," he whispered.

I obeyed, my breath hitching.

"Part your lips."

I did so on a moan.

And then he was kissing me, his breath hot and minty, his lips so very soft. It was a chaste kiss, just the barest hint of his tongue sweeping along my bottom lip. I had to force myself to not respond, just accept what he was willing to give me.

When he pulled away, I opened my eyes and muttered, "Thank you, sir."

"That's just a little taste of what you can expect if you are a good boy and please me," he purred.

"Yes, sir." I beamed.

He laughed and retreated, hopping into his car. "I'll be waiting to hear from you tomorrow."

I didn't get a chance to respond. Gabriel pulled away, his Camaro roaring down the street. Just as he had said, I knew if I was good and did everything as he required, I could expect more kisses like that. I smiled dumbly. A small part of me still thought this was a dream, that him burning the rubber off his wheels was me waking up... but the aches in my body convinced me otherwise.

"Joey? Honey, is that you?"

I turned my attention to Aunt Hanny, who was peering through the screen door. The first thing I thought was, had she seen what had happened? Had she seen an older *man* just kiss me? Did she even care? I opened my mouth to respond, but nothing came out, so I climbed the stairs.

She smiled at me as she held the door open. "You didn't text me today, so I was a little worried."

"Sorry, Auntie. I, ah... forgot." Which was the truth.

She seemed placated. "I guess I'm going to have to relax a little. You're no longer a boy."

Her words were ironic to me. I was thinking that exact same thing. I simply shrugged and followed her into the house.

"I wasn't sure what time you'd be home or if you'd eaten or not, but there is a burger in the fridge. You just have to dress it yourself," she said, wiping the counter down.

I smiled at her even though she couldn't see me. It felt great to be loved, to know there was someone out there who had sacrificed their own happiness to make sure a little boy had gotten everything he needed. It was a shame I hadn't realized it earlier. I felt so much more comfortable in my own skin now, as if the rough lining had been ground down, leaving a perfect, smooth surface. There was just one bump....

Steeling myself, I said in a shaky voice, "Auntie, I'm... gay."

I watched in trepidation as she stiffened. She turned to regard me, and I prepared myself for the questions that were surely to follow. *Are you sure? How do you know?* Instead, she grinned and said, "I know, baby."

The sound of my jaw clanking to the ground startled me. "W-what? How...?"

She sighed, apparently happy. "There were signs. I just wish you would have told me sooner."

I shook my head, unable to comprehend anything. I bit my lip and asked sheepishly, "Ah… what… signs?"

"Well!" she said on a huff. "Let's see. For starters, if you're not going to make your own bed, I suggest that you don't hide your dirty magazines under the mattress. Not to mention, I've caught you several times staring at our neighbor's son. Oh, and what straight man in his life would ever watch *RuPaul's Drag Race*?"

I blushed at every word and cursed to myself. Geez, some of those magazines were downright kinky. I looked at her, abashed. "I thought I had deleted that episode."

She gave a little giggle and shrugged. "You know the box is a little screwy."

I smacked myself in the forehead and groaned. Things were moving so quickly now. I couldn't believe I was nineteen, soon to be twenty, and that I was starting college tomorrow. Or that Hanny had known all this time about my orientation, and Gabriel…. I had found my place in this world.

I looked into my aunt's baby blues as she came up to me and wrapped me in her arms. I set my head against her shoulder and sighed.

"Did you honestly think I wouldn't approve?" she asked tenderly.

I couldn't respond.

I heard her smile on a breath. "If you weren't grown, I'd take you over my knee for ever thinking such a thing. And no matter how old you are, you'll always be my baby boy."

I couldn't help it. I grinned until my cheeks hurt. When she held me at arm's length, she frowned and touched the collar around my neck.

"Is this some sort of fashion statement?" she inquired.

I hadn't thought about how I'd explain it to her or anyone else. Gabriel had said he'd keep my role confidential, and I figured that would apply to me as well. I may have been able to tell her I was gay, but how do you explain to someone you love you are a sex slave? Could she even comprehend it? I supposed that was why it was usually kept secret....

I managed to pull an excuse out of my ass. "Ah… it's more of a political statement, Auntie. There's this club… an animal rights club, and until the senseless slaughter of strays is stopped, they have taken to wearing collars. Um… they kinda asked me if I wanted to join and, yeah…."

She gasped in delight and kissed me on the cheek. "That's a wonderful idea. I'm so proud of you!"

I smiled dumbly, surprised she had bought it. She was usually very suspicious of my clumsy explanations. In any case, I was glad with the way things were working out. My mind was still blown by the fact that she had known I was gay all this time and had treated me just the same.

"Auntie, I never… I never said thank you," I managed, the swirl of emotions making me dizzy.

Her eyes teared up, and she crushed me to her again. "There is nothing to thank me for. We take care of each other."

I smiled. "Yes, ma'am."

I supposed that was true. For as long as I could remember, it had always been about me and my needs. She'd never had anyone other than a few friends, no boyfriends, and I wished she would find someone she could share her life with. I supposed that in a way she had. She had always been there for me, watching with prideful eyes and smiles that rivaled the sun.

"Well—" She patted my cheek. "—in any event, tomorrow is your big day."

"Yeah." I nodded. "I can't wait. I think I'm just going to head to bed and get a good night's rest."

"I think that's a good idea." She smiled and kissed me on the cheek for the umpteenth time. "I'll make you a big breakfast in the morning, and you will eat every bit of it."

"Okay, Auntie." I smiled and slipped away as she started fiddling with something.

When I got to my room, I collapsed on the bed. I felt so good, light, as if everything were neatly in its place. I dug out the contract from my backpack and looked it over. It wasn't something that was legally binding, but more of a promise between two people. It made our relationship more real in a way, set down rules and such. I supposed in a vanilla relationship there was a lot of awkwardness and fear of the unknown, but the contract made me feel... level. I knew what I could expect from him. I just prayed I could live up to his expectations.

I traced his signature with my fingers, the script so elegant. I decided to leave the contract close to me and stuck it in my bedside table. I emptied the rest of my backpack, tossing an unused pair of socks back in my drawer. When I reached back in, my fingers touched something hard and bumpy.

I pulled out the little white book Gabriel had given me. I'd never kept a diary before. I opened it to the first page. My eyes fell to a set of digits on the back of the cover. It wasn't Gabriel's number, but the area code was local. It took me a few seconds, but I guessed this was Timothy's number. Gabriel had said he would pass it along to me.

Biting my lip, I retrieved my cell phone and hesitated. It wasn't super late, but I wasn't sure of the man's schedule. He could be occupied at Mistress Victoria's residence, for all I knew. I decided to take a chance anyway.

It only rung once before a familiar voice answered.

"Timothy at your service," he said suavely.

"Ah... hi... this is, ah, Joey?" I stumbled.

"Oh! Hey, how's it going?" he said, his cheerful voice making me smile.

"So good!" I cleared my throat. "Sorry... really well. I, ah... we signed a contract."

"No. Shit. That's just great. I had a feeling you would. Not just because Gabriel is frickin' sexy as hell, but you rubbed me as the true slave type."

I couldn't help but squirm a little. "Am I that easy to read?"

"Yes and no. It's just the impression I got. Hanging around all the clubs and Mistress Victoria's pad, you sorta develop a sixth sense, know what I mean? You have the subs that have no problem submitting to a master during play, but then you have the true slaves. Almost like *It*."

I started sweating, my stomach tumbling.

Timothy laughed. "That's not what I meant. I realize the whole concept of nonconsensual slavery is still shocking to you. Who knows? Maybe I'm wrong, and you might find that the 24-7 thing isn't for you, but if I'm right, that doesn't make you an *It*."

I sighed and couldn't help the words spilling from my lips. "I liked being with Gabriel all the time, not just servicing him, but doing chores for him and helping him with little things. He seems to hold a certain respect for me, and I can't describe the feeling I get when he tells me how happy he is with me. I don't know.... What if one day he wants me to...?"

"Here's an idea, Joey. Nonconsensual slavery doesn't make you an *It*, so stop associating the two with each other. Do you know George? The guy that was handling the cars that night? He is consensual only, has been for ten years, yet Mistress Victoria treats him the same as *It*. Do you want my advice?"

"Yes, please."

"Focus on you. If what you want is to please Gabriel, then that's what you do. If you feel that his preference doesn't match your own, then you move on. It's all about finding the right person whose needs match yours. Should you find that some of your needs aren't being fulfilled, you should let Gabriel know. It's the same issue that didn't make our relationship work. Needless to say, it's very important to find the right person. Doms tend to have very specific tastes that fulfill them. It's no different for a sub."

I let the man's words soak in. Remarkably, separating the concept of *It* from nonconsensual slavery did wonders to reinforce my confidence in my relationship with Gabriel. It was so simple a concept it was a wonder why I didn't think of it before.

"Can I ask why you and Gabriel didn't, ah... work out?" I inquired, wanting to know.

"Well, I wouldn't necessarily say we didn't work out. We both knew going in that there was no 'forever.' I wanted the experience of 24-7 slavery, and he had no one at the time. I'm an out and proud pain slut, but Gabriel doesn't like to punish unless earned. He has his sadistic side, no doubt, but there's a limit to it. In the beginning, I had started purposely disobeying and racking up points just to earn punishment. He had picked up on it pretty quickly and would ban me from attention when I misbehaved—that man's intuition is freaky. The more points I earned, the less pain he gave me. I guess you could say we just weren't a match, although I have no regrets about the time we spent together and enjoyed it very much. He's a really good guy, and you should feel lucky to have someone like him introduce you to the lifestyle."

I took a deep breath and closed my eyes. "I really do. Sometimes, it doesn't feel real."

"It's usually like that in the beginning." Timothy laughed. "You just have to be honest with him and yourself about what you *need*."

I laughed morosely. "I already botched that part."

I explained to Timothy about my big omission and how I thought it was all over the night Gabriel had dropped me off. It felt good talking about it to someone who could understand—who shared my own kinks and had possibly experienced such things. He listened intently as I detailed how Gabriel had given me a second chance and had punished me afterward. Strangely, I didn't feel awkward admitting to Timothy that I had let a man take me over his knee and spank me like a misbehaving child.

"The guy is really good for that—working things out. I'm surprised he didn't go into the medical field. He would have made one helluva shrink. I'm glad it worked out for you, but don't do it again. Trust him to guide you," he said, his smile coming through the phone. "He's going to push you hard starting now, if only to learn your limits. He did the same to me, although finding my limits took a lot of effort. I do have a few, but I'm pretty lenient in what I let a Dom do to me—I'm talking too much about myself."

"No, it's okay," I said adamantly. "I mean, I've watched porn and read stories, but hearing real-life experiences makes it... more real, I guess."

"That's good. You know, you can call me anytime to talk, if you need. Like Gabriel, I had no one to talk to about the shit in my head, so I know how alienated you've probably felt these past few years."

I nodded and sighed. "I've never really had any friends, just some high school acquaintances. I wasn't very popular in high school, and I sure as shit can't talk to my aunt about this. Thank you so much, really."

"No problem, my man. I was in the same boat as you back in high school. I was a football hero, had a girlfriend and everything, but no matter how popular I was, I still felt alone. I even resorted to bullying other kids because it was what I was expected to do—and it made me feel better. There was a little nerd with big glasses and bad acne I was cruel to. I'd give anything to find him and apologize. I would do anything to tell him that it wasn't him who was the problem, but me. Back then, being gay wasn't accepted as it is today, and I don't need to mention how BDSM was for the 'bad people.' I had hated myself back then, hated the things I thought about at night. Shit... Gabriel always said I talk too much."

"It's okay." I smiled and teased. "I like being talked to."

"Damn. I offered you an ear, but I didn't think I might get one in return. You're good peeps, Joey," he said, and I thought he might be tearing up a little.

178

"There was one other thing I wanted to ask, if I could?" I pushed.

"Shoot."

"I, ah, Gabriel told me that his last boy had died? I was just wondering…."

"Yeah… he got with Tam a few months after our contract was up. Did you know I'm older than Gabe? Anyway… I think that's something for him to explain, but he took it pretty hard. I'm really happy he's found someone to serve him. There is one thing I can tell you. He needs a slave as much as a slave needs him. He's not the type of person who does well alone, if you know what I mean. Honestly, I was getting a little worried that he hadn't taken a new boy after all this time."

I wasn't sure how to respond to that. I wanted to know the details but didn't know how to ask Gabriel, but Timothy's admission spoke volumes. "Thanks, I just don't want to pry."

"Take my earlier advice and focus on you right now. When the time comes, I'm sure it will be revealed. Hey, I'd love to sit on the phone with you all night and bullshit, but I got some stuff to do. Call me anytime, though, okay?"

"Thank you, so much!" I practically shouted, feeling buoyant.

He chuckled and bid me a good-night.

I sighed and set my new diary on top of the contract. I cracked my window and let the cool night air in, then quickly shed my clothes. I lay on top of my sheets, the buttery light from my closet spilling out. I replayed our conversation in my head. A lot of what he had said made sense, and I felt as if I'd just made my first ever friend at a new school. Although I felt a connectedness with Gabriel, I felt a kinship with Timothy. We were on the same side, both subs. I knew I could count on the man to be there if I had a concern about something.

Maybe one day my relationship with Gabriel would progress to nonconsensual slavery, but if it didn't, that would be okay. And if we somehow just weren't right for one another, that was okay too. I had to admit that I was suffering from "love at first sight." Gabriel was my first relationship, and fantasies of it never ending ran rampant in my head, but that was not reality. Score two for another part of growing up, I mused. I'd take Timothy's advice and focus on what I needed from Gabriel, and accept all he had to teach me. We might not make it as a couple, but I didn't doubt we'd somehow always be in each other's life.

I never thought I could feel this good, this... complete.

I felt amazing, in fact, comfortable in my body, and my hand trailed down my abdomen.

As my cock stirred, I laughed to myself. Nope, not happening. I would not disobey Gabriel. I knew I could and would probably get away with it, but that would destroy everything our new relationship meant. I wanted to submit to him, and I knew I had to come to terms with the full meaning of that. I didn't think I quite understood it yet, but I was looking forward to exploring it.

I folded my arms behind my head and stared at my ceiling.

This was just the beginning.

NIK VALENTINE lives in Chicago with their mew, Olly, and pooch, Danni. They have been writing since a young age, filling up notebooks with ramblings and naughty things. When they're not writing, they love checking out the club scene and generally getting into things they shouldn't.

E-mail Nik at NikValentine3@gmail.com.

Also from DREAMSPINNER PRESS

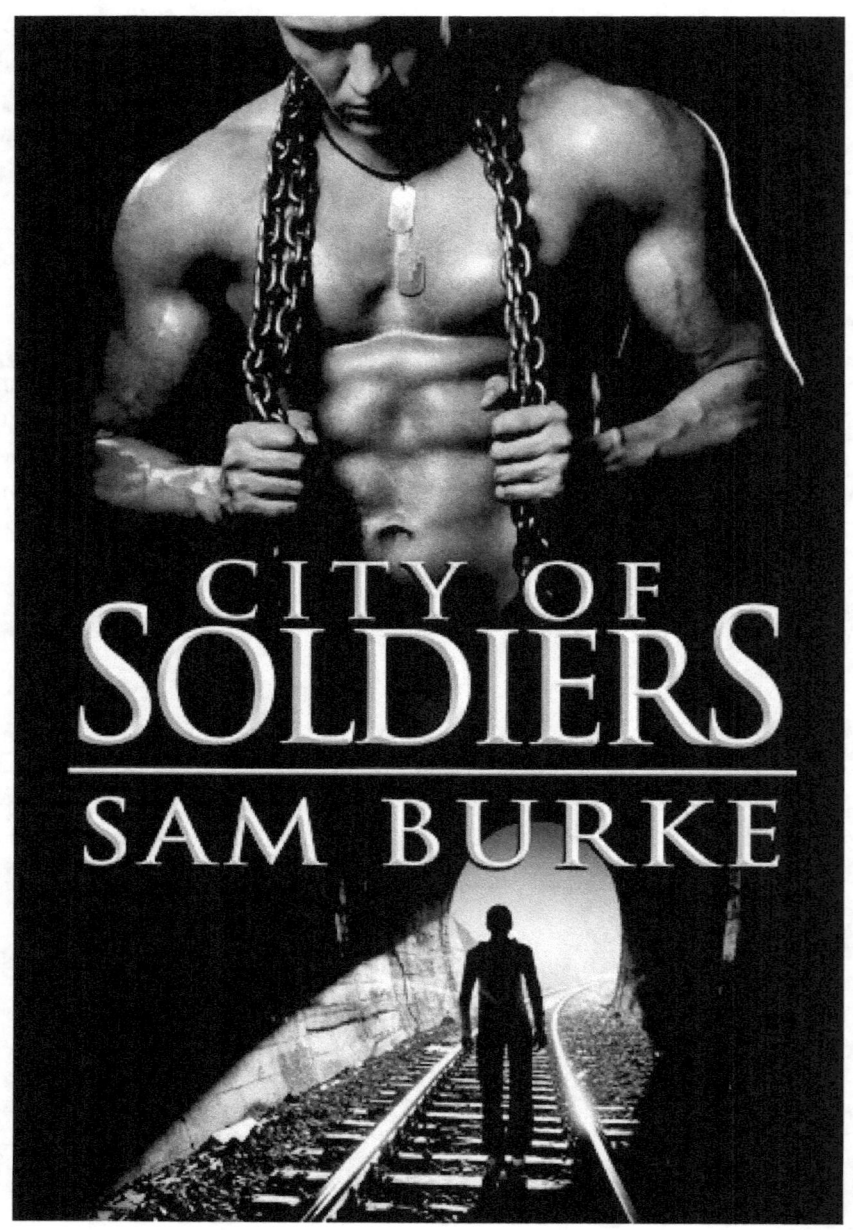

http://www.dreamspinnerpress.com

A GUARDS OF FOLSOM NOVEL

SJD PETERSON

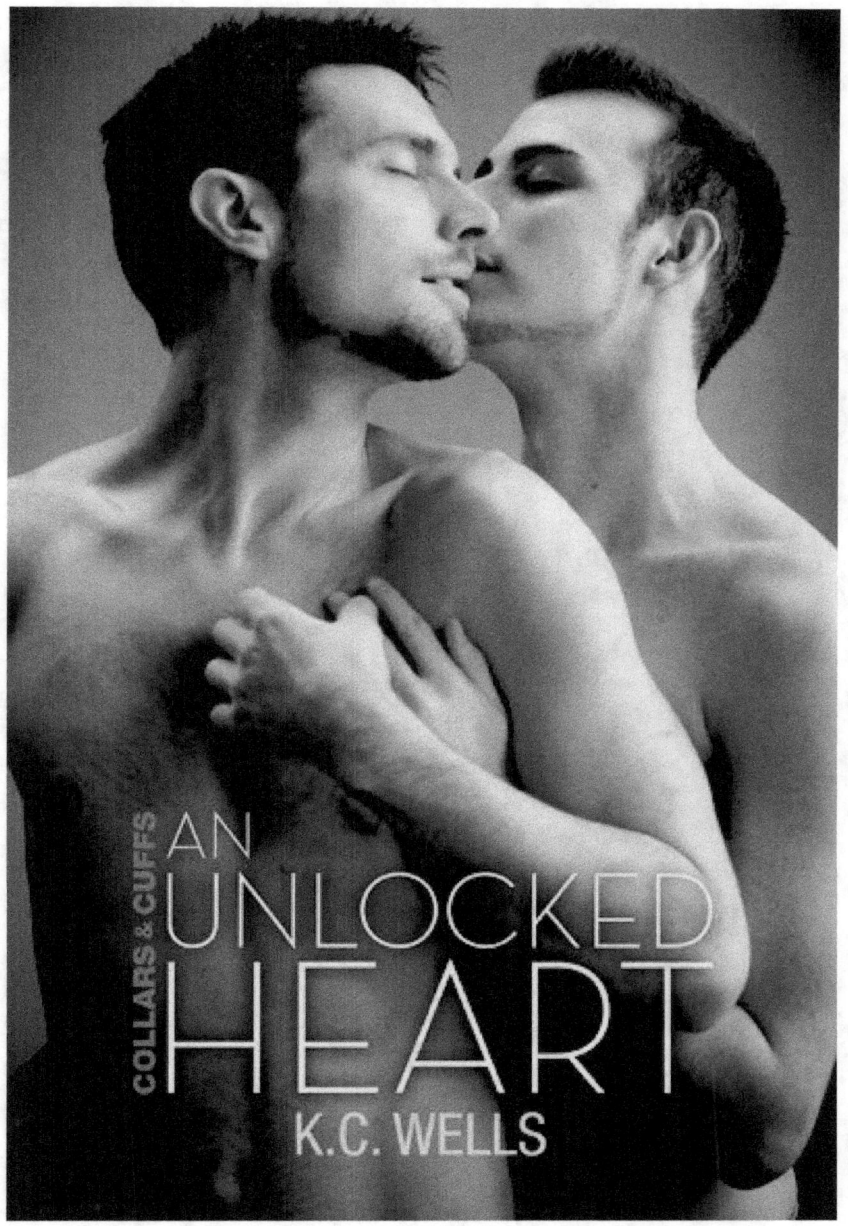

Leather + Lace

A.B. GAYLE

Also from DREAMSPINNER PRESS

Tia Fielding

Falling
into
Place

http://www.dreamspinnerpress.com

www.ingramcontent.com/pod-product-compliance
Lightning Source LLC
Chambersburg PA
CBHW060059260626
47160CB00005B/1726